DOUBLE PARKED IN THE TWILIGHT ZONE

SUMMER OF 1960

Carl Addison Swanson

outskirtspress
DENVER, COLORADO

This is a work of fiction. The events and characters described herein are imaginary and are not intended to refer to specific places or living persons. The opinions expressed in this manuscript are solely the opinions of the author and do not represent the opinions or thoughts of the publisher. The author has represented and warranted full ownership and/or legal right to publish all the materials in this book.

Double Parked in the Twilight Zone
Summer of 1960

v3.0

Cover Image by Carl A. Swanson.

Outskirts Press, Inc.
http://www.outskirtspress.com

ISBN: 978-1-4787-0495-9

PRINTED IN THE UNITED STATES OF AMERICA

TO A WORM IN HORSERADISH,
THE WORLD IS HORSERADISH

Chapter 1

They told me that I had to write all this stuff down and it would help me. I didn't much believe them but I am doing it anyhow. It is tough being a twelve year old kid who looks like Alfred E. Newman complete with big ears, freckles and a gap between my two front teeth. I come from the town of Westport which is a rich place in Connecticut near New York City. That probably doesn't mean much to you because you've never heard of it. It was named an All-American City a couple of years ago and there are some pretty famous movie stars living here. There are also a lot of rich assholes living here so maybe you don't want to hear about it. But one of the reasons I am in this psycho place is Westport cuz if you are ugly, poor or uncoordinated in Westport you are dead meat especially if you are a goofball who looks like Alfred E. Newman like me.

My whole sad ass story starts with the end of school in 6th grade. I went to Bedford Elementary School in an old concrete building from the Jeffersonian architectural period. The school sits up on a big hill just a short ways from downtown. The downtown area ain't much but small shops. The river is close to Main Street and is pretty wide. It makes for some damn good postcards if you like that sort of thing. I guess you would call it a "pretty" town if you were a girl or some snot nosed rich person. I like it because the YMCA is downtown.

Sixth grade is sort of a big deal in Westport. They have a graduation and you move on to junior high where some people actually smoke for real and girls wear bras and you have more than one teacher. Of course in Westport they make a pretty big deal about everything so maybe I just figure 6th grade is a big deal when it is just a small deal among many other small big deals. I hope you follow my meaning because I am not sure I do. What you only really need to know is that they have a lot of stuff going on here involving us kids.

During 4th period right after lunch, I was handed a note from the principal to meet with Guidance Counselor Wiggins. "Ole Wiggy" as he was called was an old man everyone liked but who gave everyone the creeps. He always wore a cardigan sweater with a black tie and red shirt. No exceptions. He would have been the brunt of many jokes and snide remarks but Ole Wiggy was a fairly nice man. I had the misfortune of meeting with him almost weekly. The reason being was I was a goofball and in most of my teachers' opinions I lacked "motivation". This was not acceptable in a town such as Westport because excellence was the prime motive of the school system and the expectations of many overachieving parents. Since my father had gone to Harvard way back in 1932 and my mother also had a college degree from a place called McGill around 1937, they joined the flock of sweaty parents worried about their kids' futures. Parents did a lot of worrying here about their kids. It was really an obsession. I just learned that word here at the hospital so I am going to use it.

As I strolled slowly from my art class to Ole Wiggy's office, the civil defense drill alarm bell went off. This was no ordinary bell. Much different than a fire alarm bell sound, this alarm had an eerie type of echo to it almost like a French police car yelping in the movies. Since I knew these drills were of no use whatsoever because the Russians would surely hit New York City first and destroy Westport in the process, I decided to opt for Ole Wiggly instead of the fallout shelter in Bedford's smelly basement. Most of the teachers used the drill to smoke a cigarette in the fallout shelter anyhow. The kids weren't allowed to talk. It was real stinky and dull.

Ole Wiggly's office was on the second floor of the old building. I carefully walked past Principal

"Chrome Dome" Flynt's office. I had seen enough of the old gizzard this year. His secretary was puffing away on a Lucky Strike in her office and she smiled at me probably happy it was my last day under her domain. I tapped softly on the glass door of Wiggly's office. It was imprinted with a bold "Guidance Counselor" warning on its shiny beveled glass window.

"Who goes there?" A voice from within said.

"It's me."

"Who's me?"

"Justin Carmichael, sir."

"Enter, Squire Fletcher Justin." Wiggly liked to talk like that. "Master" or "Squire" was used quite often by the ole guy. My given name was Fletcher Justin Carmichael. To everyone, I was Justin. Thank God. My mother said my name was lucky. She taught Latin at one time and seemed to know many such odd things.

I opened the door. It was heavy, loaded with authority. The office was small with a banquet table serving as a desk. Papers and books were everywhere with no order. My immediate thought was my mother would never approve of Wiggly's organization skills.

"What can I do for you, Justin?" The voice said. I did not see him.

"Where are you, sir?" I asked. My father had been an officer in the Navy during World War II. "Sir" and "Ma'am" were to be used in respect of elders. Certainly Wiggly qualified.

"I am here." Wiggly said. He was standing on his head in the corner by the radiator. His shoes had been removed and his shirt had fallen from his pants.

"Why are you standing on your head?"

"Why are you here?"

"I asked first." For a goofball I had a quick mouth. More often than not it got me in trouble.

Wiggly flipped his feet down like he knew what he was doing. He landed in a crouched position and pushed his long hair away from his face. It was the first time I had seen him without his glasses. He looked younger if that was possible for a man who had to be . . . nearly sixty years old.

"There is a civil defense drill going on. Why are you not responding?" He asked fixing his hair with both hands and reaching for his glasses.

"I would rather be here, sir."

"Well, you are not going to like what I have to say."

"Do I ever?" I asked with a slight smirk on my face.

"You are a bright young man, Justin. I like you. I don't like many of your classmates, you know. Very tiresome lot this year especially. You seem to grow up so quickly these days."

"Yes, sir."

"Oh, for God's sake, Justin. Stop that military jargon. Call me Ole Wiggly like everyone else does behind my back."

"Really?"

He laughed. "You kids are so gullible. It is a good thing I am not a teacher."

"I thought you were once?"

Wiggly adjusted his wire rim glasses. He got serious with a slight frown on his face.

"Sit down, Justin."

"Yes, sir."

"Now I have to give you the lecture about why you are such a goofball. You know I don't much like telling you this time and time again, but it is my job. I want you to know however that your generation is very lucky. You are lucky to be free of war and to live in an age of innocence. One day you will look back at this time and realize how you squandered such a perfect opportunity to be . . . well . . .to be happy."

The lecture wasn't long enough. I had to go to the basement "fallout shelter "where the Civil Defense Drill was still being conducted. The basement of Bedford Elementary was separated into about five rooms. The crummy room where my class was stationed smelled like my grandfather's house. Old, damp and musty. My teacher Mrs.

Weiman gave me a nod as I entered the dimly lit area. She pretended not to be smoking but I could see the cigarette in her right hand. My classmates huddled in the far right corner next to a concrete wall supposedly built to withstand Russian nuclear radiation. It was really stupid to pretend that was so, as was the entire process of the drills. But I must say it did have an effect on all of us though. It scared the living tar out of us.

"What did Ole Wiggly want?" Brian Hodges asked. Hodges was my good friend and a fellow member of the Marauders, our Little League team.

"He was standing on his head."

"Really?" Hodges asked. The others sat bored. Boys by the left wall and girls by the far wall. This was the last day of school. Any news about Ole Wiggly was old news.

I didn't answer Brian. I sat down next to Joannie Olson and put my head between my knees. She was a freckled face red head I knew from Ms. Comer's dance class.

"You okay, Justin?" She asked. Joannie always seemed to care about people to their face and then she would stab them in the back. I was not gonna let on that I was down. I couldn't really figure out why I was so unhappy. Ole Wiggly had given me the damn lecture before about how I was a goofball and my teachers, parents and everybody in damn Westport thought I could do better if I tried. My grades weren't really that bad but since I could do well on their stupid IQ tests I was considered an "underachiever." Also I had a brother, Duff, who was like a genius. Everybody loved him and he was two grades ahead of me. It ain't easy following some guy like that. Actually he was a complete jackass. I knew that real well.

The drill alarm finally went off and we started to head back to class. The Russians hadn't bombed the hell out of us that day. I walked with Brian and my other buddy, Steve Oliver. Steve was smaller than me if you can believe that and had a healthy pair of ears on him too. But nobody seemed to tease him much probably because he had some really good looking older sisters who dated some really big guys. Being big was a big factor in overcoming being ugly, poor or uncoordinated in Westport. If you could fight nobody messed with you.

"Who are you gonna dance with at graduation?" Brian asked. The graduation and dance wasn't for two days but Brian was the sort of guy who worried a lot about stuff like that.

"Joannie." Steve answered confidently. I never saw what he saw in her but it was his choice and he was much more experienced with girls than me. I mean he was always making out like crazy at parties and all. He was a regular kissing maniac. He really was.

"How about you, Justin?" Everyone knew Brian had a big crush on Joannie, so Steve's comment must have stung.

"Maybe I will just dance with Betsy Firestone," I replied. I knew this would cause some guys to roll their eyes because Betsy was probably the cutest girl in the class and everybody loved her.

But nobody did. Maybe I did have a chance?

Chapter 2

Our first Little League game, played on a week day was that night. Baseball always made me feel better. My mother sensed I was down and made me a special dinner of pizza. My father was often traveling in some far off country doing whatever he did so we could live so great in Westport. He did some kind of work with rubber plants in other countries. He had a big long title which I never could remember but it sounded very important. When my father traveled, my mother served us some real cool stuff: Pizza or Chinese take-out. On this particular night Duff was off on some Pilgrim Fellowship trip through the church. I am not a big fan of religion, I gotta tell you. That probably makes me a heathen headed for hell but I find it pretty boring. The sermons are enough to kill you. Whatever, my brother had a lot of friends in this church group which I found to be totally dorky but there were some good looking girls in it. I must say that. Otherwise, forget it.

"Who are you playing tonight?" My mother asked. She puffed on her Pall Mall while driving with both hands. The new Ford Country Squire station wagon was a big car and my mother was not a good driver. At least my father kept telling her so. She would suddenly stomp on the brakes nearly sending me through the front window or she would tailgate the car in front of her. She was really a maniac behind the wheel of a car.

"The Cardinals."

"That's Bobby Mathews's team, right?"

"Yep."

"Do you have contact with Bobby anymore?" She asked. Mathews had been on my minor league team and we were close then. But when they re-districted us to Bedford Elementary and he stayed at Coleytown we had little to say to each other when we saw one another. That happened more than often with Mathews. It was very strange to me how you could be friends one day and then the next barely talk to one another. Odd how friendships sort of do that. I mean you may be great buddies but be away for any time at all and it changes. And I didn't think I had changed at all.

"No, Mom. He still goes to Coleytown and will go to Long Lots next year. He is now the enemy."

"I wish you boys wouldn't take sports so seriously. It isn't with your brother." If I had heard that statement one time I had heard it a thousand times. My brother was always the ideal. The good guy. I was always the goofball taking crap from everyone. It was a serious issue to me.

"He isn't into sports like me."

"He gets good grades."

"That's because he is a brownnoser. Thanks for the ride, Mom."

"Oh, I am going to come and watch."

Funny the only other time she had come to one of my games was when Kirk Douglas showed up to watch his son, Michael, play on my minor league team the Cubs. The same team Bobby Mathews had played on. Both my brother and I were on that team and we were really pretty good. My brother was the star pitcher and I played a good second baseman. Kirk wouldn't show up too much because he was out in Hollywood making big money in movies. But when he did, all the mothers would show up for sure. Michael wasn't so hot a player. He played center field which is sort of like a low life on a Little League team. So I guess Kirk didn't show up a lot because his son wasn't so hot and considering he was a big hot shot actor he probably didn't want to watch a lousy center fielder.

The Marauders were a good team with a sort of goofy name. I am not sure where that name came from and I actually never asked. It was one of those things that goofballs like me never thought about. But we were the defending Westport American League champions and proud of it. I played shortstop and was a leadoff batter. I was excellent at fielding but not much of a batter. I reasoned that came from basically being afraid of being hit in the head by the ball. This "worry gene" was inherited from my father who worried about everything. Instead of the mere "earmuff" protective helmets used by most players, my father had bought me a plastic helmet with an earflap for complete protection. Even still I was scared of being hit and would duck down as the pitch approached. Many times I was so small, this would limit my strike zone to a matter of inches and I would readily walk. This was fine with me and Coach Hotchinson, our manager. So in that sense I was quite a valuable player to the Marauders. I could field like Tony Kubek of the Yankees and get on base a lot. I really could hit. In practice games I could slug the ball to the outfield. In games though, that "Carmichael chicken gene" made me scared.

Bobby Mathews was the Cardinals' pitcher that day, as in most of the games. In Little League if you had one strong pitcher, you worked him like a dog.

If you didn't have a good pitcher, your team usually stank. Bobby threw sidearm. He came from the right side and the ball usually came directly at the batter and curved toward the plate. That is, if his curve was working. If it wasn't working, Bobby's pitches hit a lot of batters and this made me scared as hell. I bailed out twice and struck out both times. With the score 3-2 our favor in the bottom of the fifth inning, I came to bat. I took a quick look to see my mother puffing away on a Pall Mall and talking up a storm with several women. She hated sports, except for golf, and I wondered why she had even come to see the game. I guess she had nothing much else to do with my father gone and all. She often was pretty lonely, I think. I dug in the batter's box this time determined to stand up to Mathews' sidearm delivery.

The first pitch was a high ball. I stepped out to see Coach Corrigan at third base give me the bunt sign. I checked again. There was nobody on base. I looked again and he made the sign again . . . once to the nose and then the right ear meant bunt. I rolled my eyes and dug back into the batter's box. Mathews threw me a ball inside just as I turned to bunt. My entire body faced the pitcher's mound and the oncoming baseball. When it was clearly too late, my body attempted to collapse. But as I did that the baseball hit me right in the crotch. To most players this would be a disaster. However, they were not Carmichaels. In our family we wore jock straps with steel cones. Better safe than sorry, my father would say. So with the helmet covering my head and the steel girder covering my privates, I could have been playing football.

There was a deafening sound heard throughout Coleytown Little League field. It was the sound of a hard leather ball hitting pure steel hidden in my jock strap. The sound echoed off the front windows of Mrs. Wolfsom's third grade classroom on the eastern side of the elementary school. A few spectators held their ears. It was much like the Civil Defense Drill alarm. As I lay in the dirt of the batter's box my body in a fetal position, I heard people yelling from my dugout.

"Run, Justin! Run!"

As I peered up from the dust, I saw the Cardinals' left fielder running madly for the ball which seemed destined for the left field fence. I came to the sudden realization that most people in the park thought I had actually hit the ball with the bat instead of my steel testicle protector propelling the baseball. I was tempted to get up and run but the idea that I could have actually been hurt drained me emotionally. I was spent. I lay there in mental agony. Soon there was a crowd around me. My mother was there as well and everyone was very sympathetic while they were staring at my crotch. As I limped off the field in an orchestrated dragging of my feet as two teammates carried me, I got a thoughtful applause from the spectators. I looked about and my eyes caught sight of a small figure on the bleachers near third base.

It was Betsy Firestone.

Chapter 3

Bedford Elementary School's graduation and dance was held the following night at the crummy school. I shouldn't really call it crummy but it was old and named after some ole Westporter. Coleytown was much nicer and newer. I am not sure who decided to change my school but he must have been some kind of dummy. The only good thing about Bedford was that it was close to downtown and the YMCA. Us guys went down there every afternoon and played pool, ping pong, basketball and swam. It was a great place. They even had dances there sometimes on Friday nights. The last one I went to was with Joannie Olson. Since she was eye balling Hodges all night, I decided to give her the cold shoulder. I barely spoke to her most of the night. Didn't do me much good though. Joannie could be real nasty.

My mother declined going to the graduation because the game had been enough excitement for her for a month. It is not every day your son gets hit in the steel jock strap after all. So I got a ride from my neighbor and fellow classmate, Michael Babkie. Michael was my best friend away from school. This is hard to explain but Michael, never Mike, was sort of a dork. He looked much like Dennis the Menace and even had a strand of hair sticking up on his blond head. During the summer months we were inseparable but during school we went our separate ways. It was odd in a way but we both understood why. I was cool and Michael was not. It was that simple. He was good looking, a fair athlete and the Babkies were hardly poor but Westport required a tad more clever sarcastic wit to run with the cool crowd. And Michael did not possess such an ability. I however could be a silver tongued devil. That was the key to being popular in school. You had to have a quick mind and a smart mouth. My mind was not that smart or anything but I can run off some knee knocking "cuts" to guys or girls if I needed to. Plus I usually had a nickname for everybody which was also sort of knocking them but they really didn't realize it. Like for instance I called this one girl "Hawkeye" because she wore these huge thick glasses. I guess it wasn't very nice but I could be sort of mean at times. It was really what was needed to survive in Westport. It was a dog-eat-dog town I gotta tell you.

"I heard you got hit in the balls during the game last night,." Michael said while sitting in the back seat of his father's Cadillac on the way to graduation. Now most of us kids called these cars "Jew canoes" or "Rabbi roadsters" but since the Babkies weren't Jewish we didn't go there.

"Who told you?" I asked lost for a moment in thought.

"Your mother told my mother."

Jeez! Women, I thought to myself. Why would my mother tell anybody about that? I suddenly got a pain in my stomach. I wondered if Betsy had told anybody.

Papa Joe Babkie dropped us off at the school without a word. He was a big Polish man who rarely spoke. Once when I tripped Michael's brother into a pile of dog shit Michael and I got into a fight. The next day there was a punching bag in the Babkie's garage with my face on it. Needless to say Babkie's parents were not wild about me.

"See you, Michael," I said, heading for the gym.

"Who you gonna dance with?" He asked. For some unknown reason, Micheal was not popular with the girls. He was shy and he didn't know how to dance. He would most likely sit in the corner of the gym alone. He did have a crush on Patti Driscoll who was sort of cool but he never talked with her or anything. Some boys were just as strange as girls.

"Betsy Firestone! " I answered him in a loud roar.

"Good luck!" he yelled back at me in a doubtful tone as I skipped down the side stairs.

The gym was decorated with balloons and streamers. Everything was in blue and white which were Bedford Elementary's colors. There was a stage set for the parents and teachers at one end of the gym. To be honest, it was sort of cheesy looking considering this was Westport. Chairs were lined up in front of the stage for us students. I sat down in the last row as was my custom in any school function or class. Hodges was already there in his madras jacket and tie. I had decided to wear a sweater and no tie. I hate ties. They might be the dumbest invention ever thought of for men. Maybe a woman invented them. Kids began filing in by the dozens and I noticed Betsy in a cute white dress with a belt. She was decidedly small with a cute pug nose and straight brown hair. She also had great eyes. She was the kind of girl you looked at and smiled. Every boy at Bedford Elementary had a crush on her but she was not the kind of girl who knew it.

Betsy's father was the principal over at Coleytown Elementary, my old school, before

Bedford Elementary. He was a short man with a solemn face and glasses that made his head look smaller. He didn't smile much but after our few sessions together over my misbehavior, he was an okay guy. It didn't hurt that his daughter was beautiful. But I didn't know Betsy then so he was okay with or without a cute daughter.

"Welcome to the 1960 graduation of the senior class of Bedford Elementary School," Principal Flynt announced. His bald head reflected the age old Christmas lights behind him. Everybody called him "Chrome Dome" behind his back. He had suspended me once for half a day for breaking some girl's pen. Chrome Dome could be a really mean guy. I cried like hell when that happened. My mother picked me up and told me my father would understand. But he didn't. He made me rake leaves at the girl's house two weekends in a row. It was very embarrassing but I guess I deserved it. It was a crummy old pen but I shouldn't have broken it and made the girl cry.

The commencement of our class lasted forever. It was a long winded ceremony with all sorts of self-praising and bravado and made me want to throw up. I mean the teachers are good and all but I am not exactly Einstein and I did okay. They also gave out about 200 awards for everything you could think of including one for "Best Citizen." That was Benjamin Swartz, the biggest brownnoser in the class. Everyone hated him including me. I got one award: a silver medal for the gym competition. It was sort of lame but I hung it around my neck anyway. Brian Hodges got a gold one and I didn't understand that. I beat him in just about everything. It seemed like they were giving every kid an award and we had a lot of super stupid kids in our class. No offense but as Ole Mr. Wiggly had said, "this was no brain factory."

Once everyone was finished patting themselves on the back and telling everyone how great they were, there was an intermission. All the smokers made a bee line outside to puff one. If my mother had been there, I am sure she would have lit up right there on stage. She was a real chain smoker. The janitors started taking down all the chairs getting ready for the dance to follow. I saw ole George, the janitor for the 3rd floor. If you gave George a penny he would touch his nose with his tongue. No kidding. He really could do it. I guess he needed the money too. Ole George was all right. You could tell he was out of his league in a rich elementary school and all. He probably lived in a dingy old apartment in Bridgeport and took the bus to work. I liked him though. He was always smiling and kidding around. He was sort of my pal if you must know. Matter of fact I sort of like poor people. My father had this guy "Teddy" who worked on our lawn when us kids couldn't do the big stuff like cut down a tree or something. And Teddy was a super guy. He sounded a real different from me and you. I think he might have been Russian or something. But he was no Commie or anything. He was as American as me and maybe you. He was a real good worker. My father used to bring him a couple of beers at the end of his working at the house. They would sit out there on the grass and drink those cold beers. I liked to see my father do that sometimes. It made him seem like not so much of a rich guy like he acted like most times around his friends.

"Justin, come here," Brian Hodges yelled over from the corner. He was standing with Steve Oliver close together like it was some kind of secret meeting. We had actually formed a fraternity. Just the three of us. We called it the Delta Fraternity and got rings and matching jackets from Greenberg's, a clothing store downtown. Oliver suggested it because he thought it was pretty cool that one of his sisters, Pinky, was going steady with a guy in a fraternity.

"What?" I asked coming to the corner where they stood. I was still a little mad because Hodges got a gold medal and I only got a silver one. I could be pretty competitive on stuff like that.

"Listen, we think we can arrange for us all to go steady." Brian said.

"What are you talking about?"

"Steve, you tell him."

"We think that Joannie Olson wants to go steady with Brian."

"So," I said. "She certainly doesn't want me. Actually I think she is sort of a bitch."

"Hey!" Hodges said.

"Hey what? All she talked about on our date was you."

"So, what is wrong with that?"

"Nothing if it's you she's dating."

We stood, kicking at the floor. Little boys stuff. When you don't know what to do, look at the floor. Kick your feet.

"So what do you want to do?" Oliver asked.

"About what?" I asked.

"All of us going steady."

"What are you talking about?" I was dumbfounded.

"Brian will ask Joannie and she will ask Anne Daniels to go steady with me and Betsy Firestone with you."

"Are you serious?" I asked.

Brian nodded. Oliver stood his ground.

"This sounds like some kind of Chinese deal. Like when you marry your sister."

"Well, aren't we getting fussy," Hodges said.

"What is that suppose to mean?"

"You don't have to do anything, Justin. Joannie will arrange everything after she agrees to go steady with me."

"What if she says 'no' to that?"

"She ain't gonna."

I stopped for a moment. Kicked the floor some more. "Why the hell Anne Daneils, Steve? She is like two feet taller than you."

"She wears a bra."

That stumped me. No better reason I guess.

"All right, I am in," I said.

"Give me your ring," Hodges insisted.

"Oliver is going to give the rings out?"

"I am going to ask her."

"Why?" I asked.

"Because you are too chicken to ask Betsy."

He had a point there. I barely had enough nerve to talk to Betsy. And now after she saw me get hit in the balls at the game it was even worse.

I slipped off my ring at the precise moment the music started to play "Cathy's Clown" by the Everly Brothers. It was a brand new song on the charts and I knew it because my brother, the wizard dork, posted all listings on the door to his room each week. He had about 5,000 records. I liked the song though and made a dash to find Betsy.

She was sitting talking with some mother but I went over anyhow. I am not usually wild about adults I don't know but since I was going to go steady anyhow, I figured I might as well risk it.

"Excuse me, Ma'am," I said in my most convincing Eddie Haskell voice. "But would you like to dance, Betsy?"

The woman smiled. Yellow teeth like my Mom's. Betsy was blushing and I made a sort of a curtsy kidding around like we had been taught at Ms. Comer's dance class. Betsy stood up and did a curtsy back. She was super cute. I felt like crying she was so cute.

It was almost the middle of the song by the time we got to the dance floor. Not too many were dancing yet. Most of boys were standing on one side of the room, kicking the floor and looking down. The girls chatted on the other side of the auditorium.

"Are you enjoying yourself?" I asked. God, I hated to talk to girls.

"How are you feeling?" She asked and I blushed.

"Oh, I am okay."

"I guess it was lucky you were wearing something down there, huh?" Betsy said in a sort of flirting way and I just smiled. I mean she could have been a real jerk about it. Joannie Olson would have made a big joke about it.

I held her a little tighter when the song slowed down toward the end. She whispered something in my ear but I could hardly hear it.

"Say what?" I said when the music finally stopped.

"I think I have a crush on Brian Hodges," Betsy said.

Chapter 4

The next day my grandfather died.

We were all sitting around the dinner table. We always ate dinner at precisely eight o'clock. Usually my father took the train from New York City and arrived in Westport at 6:38 p.m. He would get home ten minutes later, change his clothes, have one drink and then dinner would start. It was a constant routine without change. My brother and me were usually starving to death but the refrigerator was off limits until after dinner. The conversation was very limited and mostly about the weather. My father was the son of a farmer and very concerned about the weather.

"So did you get any rain here today?" He asked.

"Nope." My mother responded.

"Did one of you boys water the lawn?" It should be understood that my father, like most

Westporters, was concerned about appearances. We may have not been very close to our neighbors but we still wanted them to think highly of us. And in this affluent suburb lawns were very important. As a result, my brother and me were slaves to our acre of grass. We fertilized it, raked the leaves off of it, mowed it in the summer and weren't allowed to play on it. It was tiresome work and often our weekend job, both Saturday and Sunday, depending on the time of the year. My father seemed to enjoy the work and he would sit at dusk and look at his lawn like an old plantation owner. It was very important to him. It made no sense to me.

"I did, Randolph." My mother said. My father was always referred to by his real name. He was never "Randy" or "Ran." Much like Michael Babkie, he was always Randolph or "Dad" to my brother and me.

"It looks like it might rain tonight," my father said, neatly fixing an equal amount of meat, potatoes and peas on his fork. He was a very disciplined man and loved routine. His mannerisms at the table were like those in his life: precise and boring. My mother once referred to him as "fuss-budget" behind his back. I never bothered to look it up in the dictionary but I bet it meant he was sort of an ass.

The phone rang. This was an unexpected moment in our household because it seldom rang and when it did, it annoyed my father.

"Who could that be?" My father asked.

"Someone calling us?" My brother dry-panned.

"Who could be calling us at this hour?" My father asked again.

"Why don't we answer it and find out?" My mother interjected.

Before being asked, my brother made a dash for the kitchen where the black rotary phone was located. We only had one phone and, if you ever wanted any privacy, you had to run the phone cord under the kitchen door and take the phone into the closet.

"Carmichael residence, this is Duff speaking, may I help you?" I heard my brother say per our father's instructions. My father was very military in these orders.

There was complete silence and although my parents continued to eat, I could tell they were listening. Nothing ever happened in our household that went without the careful supervision of my father.

My brother mumbled something and then returned to the table, his head hanging loosely from his frame.

"Well, who was it?" My father asked.

"Granddad is dead."

The ride to northern Vermont was never a great joy but this time it was terrible. We had the new station wagon, which beat the hell out of the ole Buick, but the mood was sour. My mother smoked incessantly and my father couldn't stop complaining about the traffic on Route 5. My brother was reading and I was bored.

"So, when is the funeral?" I asked.

"They told us already, bonehead," my brother said.

"Don't use those words, Duff," my mother scolded as she lit one cigarette from the other.

"He is a bone head."

"Am not!" I screamed back.

My mother turned in her seat. "Damn it!" she screamed. "Have a little respect for your grandfather!"

"Sorry, Mom. I loved Grandpa too," my brother, the eternal kiss up, babbled.

In truth, Granddad smelled like pipe tobacco and was sort of boring. He watched television endlessly. He seemed amazed at the fact a television could even work. He loved the Red Sox as did my brother. My father and I were Yankee fans. My mother could care less. My grandmother had died years ago and Granddad lived in a big

Victorian house in Northern Vermont. He once had been sort of famous I guess. He was a state senator and owned a lot of property all over the state. My mother ran his business from Westport and was pretty good at it. My father could care less. He was ten years older than my mother and I think Granddad held that against him. I am not sure why but I just got the feeling that he hated my father down deep, maybe for taking his only daughter away from him and all. Plus, he didn't like Westport at all. Thought it was the snootiest town in the United States, he once said. Granddad didn't say a lot but when he did people seemed to listen. I wouldn't mess with him. He was a pretty big guy even for an old timer.

"How much longer?" I asked. Bored.

"5 hours. Go to sleep," my father said. And I did.

The funeral was on a Saturday which seemed awkward. I was missing a baseball game. The last time I did that I lost my starting spot at short stop. Not to worry. I was an All-Star now with a set of steel balls. They had the funeral in an old church about 100 yards from my grandfather's house. It was a small town, Orleans, in Northern Vermont where everyone knew everyone. And they all turned out for my grandfather's funeral. The church was packed. My father gave the eulogy and my mother cried. It was sort of awkward knowing that my grandfather didn't like my father but I guess that is what adults do. It was sort of phony but I was beginning to realize that there was a whole bunch of phoniness going on everywhere.

My father and I left that night. My mother stayed to "take care of things" and since my brother had nothing better to do, he stayed too. So it was just Dad and me on the long ride back.

"That was a good speech you made, Dad," I said as we passed Woodstock where we usually stopped for ice cream. I wasn't pushing it today and we didn't stop.

"It is called a eulogy. And thanks," my father said. He was a pretty good driver. Not that I was an expert but I knew my mother sure wasn't any good.

"Any time," I said. "Did you mean all those things you said?"

"You mean about your grandfather?"

"Yeah, you were . . . really loving." I said. The word even surprised me.

"Your grandfather was a good man. We had our differences though."

"About what?"

He stared at me briefly and then his eyes went back to the two lane road.

"Your grandfather could be a real asshole."

Chapter 5

The very next morning, Sunday, my father woke me up early.

"We have been invited by the Shays to play golf."

"Oh, Dad, I hate George Shay."

"Tough. We tee off in an hour."

The town of Westport had purchased a private club that spring named Longshore. My father and I had actually been part of determining whether or not the town would buy the place. Herb Baldwin was the mayor of Westport and he was buddies with my father. My father wasn't really the buddy kind of guy. He wasn't really a joiner. He was stuffy and old acting. But he was pretty smart, I guess, and the mayor wanted his advice about buying a bankrupt club for 1.9 million bucks. So we went out and played it. I must tell you that the best club in my father's bag is his pencil. He is a notorious cheat in a game of cheaters. My mother can easily beat him and I can come close but when he adds up the scores at the end of the round, he is liable to have a pretty good score. You can tell a lot about someone when you play golf with them. My grandfather taught me how to play golf at the age of six so I was like a pro by now. I really was pretty good. But some guys get really mad while playing golf. Some talk all the time. Women also do that a lot on the golf course. They just keep on talking forever. Men usually take the game pretty seriously. That is why they cheat so much.

My father was waiting in the car when I hurried out of the garage and saw him pointing at me to close the door. I did so and then hopped in the station wagon.

"You got my clubs?" I asked.

"I have my clubs," he answered. Lesson time again. I was responsible for my own stuff. So I got out of the car and opened the garage door and found my bag leaning against the small cupboard in the back of the garage.

"Why do you want to play Longshore?" I asked my father after I got back in the car with my clubs.

"I need a change from the Patterson Club," my father said. He was a long time member of the tony club but recent gossip had gone around that my mother could beat him. He didn't like the ribbing he took from his playmates and thus the departure. It was one thing to be a terrible golfer. It was another to get beaten by your wife. And my mother was really, really good. I think she won the Vermont championship one year. It was sort of weird that the Patterson Club would only let her play on certain days and only in the afternoon. She complained a lot about that to my father and to the club. They didn't listen.

"I wanted to spend time with you." My father said.

"Good. Are we going to play the Shays in a match?"

"If you want?" He said.

"I want." I could be pretty competitive at some things. My brother could always whip me at board games so I never liked them. I also was pretty crummy at card games like poker or bridge so I never played them. But with home run derby or golf, bring it on. Plus, George Shay was sort of a dork. I knew I could beat him.

After nine holes, we were four up on the Shays. My father had cheated on at least two holes. He lost his ball in the woods on hole number 2, but claimed he found it when he actually dropped another. That should have taught the Shays to help him look for his ball. Then on number 7 he lost his ball in the rough and played a ball he found. It doesn't take a brain surgeon to spot the difference between a Wilson Staff and a Spalding. Since we were playing match play, my father was at free will to make up his the score. A 39 for him and a 49 for me.

"I hear you are going steady with Betsy

Firestone," George Shay said to me while we wolfed down two hot dogs at the halfway house. George was a skinny kid I had known from my Coleytown days. He wasn't cool at all but liked to think he was, if you know what I mean. He was sort of gawky looking and his pants' cuffs came up to about his knees.

"Where did you hear that?" I asked.

"Word gets around, even though you guys are at Bedford." This was true because Betsy was well known throughout the town of Westport. A legend you might say. Plus her father was the principal at Coleytown.

"Nah, I think she likes Brian Hodges."

"Everyone likes Brian," George said. He said it in a tone that made him a definite dork.

"Yep, everyone seems to," I said diplomatically.

"You ever go to any of those make-out parties?" George asked. As I already told you, George was sort of a gangly guy with long arms and legs. He had an awkward face with features too big for his head. Large ears, nose and mouth. He wasn't ugly but I knew girls didn't like him much.

"A couple," I said which was true. Westport was well advanced in the sexual experimentation department. It was not unusual for parties to include make-out sessions in the basement/dens of its lovely suburban homes. This included some music but basically long kissing was the main event. To be perfectly honest, I found them somewhat boring. Many girls were already wearing braces on their teeth and to kiss a girl with braces was disgusting, if you get my drift. I did get a constant boner, however.

"So what happens?" George pursued this line of questioning like some kind of horn dog.

"You sit and kiss all night. It really isn't all that cool, George."

"How come I never get invited?" He asked. This was like asking why someone had never been kissed before.

"You will, George. You will," I said. "Let's play some golf."

The back 9 was much the same as the first 9 holes. My father cheated like hell and the Shays basically sucked. I had a birdie on the 13th, a par 3 and my father gave me a big bear paw of a shoulder pat which was about as much touching as the Carmicheal family allowed. We weren't much for showing affection in our house. My father always gave my mother a short kiss when he came home from work, but there wasn't much hugging going on. I am not sure this was good or bad but I noticed it didn't go on much. At least not in my house. There were some spankings though.

We were all standing on the 14th tee when the protest began. Mr. Shay was a tiny man with a big beak of a nose. My father had a rather large nose himself but rarely commented on it. Considering the number of Jews in Westport it was a sensitive subject. You know the ole joke "Why do Jews have big noses? Because air is free." I never really understood the dislike for Jews though. I mean the big complaint seemed to be that they were very good at making money and very concerned about money. But so was my father and every other father in Westport, Jewish or not. So what was the big deal? The Shays were Jewish and lived in Gault Park where all the other Jews lived. We lived close by on a non-Jewish street. I think we were the only phony Protestants on the road but as long as you weren't Jewish, no one seemed to care. As I told you before, I am not real big into religion. I am probably going to hell.

"What's going on?" Mr. Shay asked. There were about 50 people parading down the fairway right at us.

My father said nothing. In Westport, you never knew what the hell was going on with protests and demonstrations. This was 1960, after all. Ike was leaving office and the entire world was going mad, according to Walter Chronkite. Blacks were demonstrating in the South, they were throwing eggs at

Vice-President Nixon in South America and everybody seemed pretty mad all the time.

"I think it is the Cockenoe Island protest march." Mr. Shay blurted out. He held his hands over the brim of his oversized hat that nearly covered his entire face. I think he may have had skin cancer at one time.

"What does that mean, Dad?" George asked, always curious. Forever asking questions.

"They want to build a nuclear power plant on Cockenoe Island." His father answered.

"Where is Cockenoe Island?" My father asked.

"Why, Randolplh, it just over there," he said pointing to our left. "It's just a mile off Compo Beach."

"Well, they can't do that. It is too dangerous." My father replied, sounding like he knew something about nuclear power plants. Maybe he did, but I doubted it. I knew when he was bluffing.

"They are going to try."

We stood on the tee unable to tee off because

of the marching crowd. Well, it was not really a crowd but certainly more than a foursome. The protestors walked right up to the front of the tee. They had banners and signs held up with long sticks explaining their protest. There were some men and women and even some young high school kids. One sort of ugly teenage girl walked right up to our tee and then took a sharp right toward the exit road where the others were heading. As she passed me, she gave me a wink and said: "Hey, Alfred." I didn't say anything back. George laughed. My father was busy with the scorecard. When they were gone my father approached the tee.

"I guess it's my honor since I got the birdie on the last hole," he snorted.

Chapter 6

My mother and brother came back 2 days later on the night of Ms. Comer's final dance recital. My mother still looked sad and my brother was still a dork. The dance was the conclusion of 6 months or more of classes every Friday night. Everyone wore formal wear including white gloves. It was held at the YMCA. I guess Westport wanted to make sure its young boys and girls grew up to be proper adults like their parents. Little did they know that make-out parties were often held the next night!

Parents were invited to the dance recital but my father was headed off to Venezuela for something and my mother said she was too tired. She wanted to go to bed early.

"I need a ride, Mom," I protested as my father jumped into the airport limo.

"Isn't Michael going?"

"You know he is not in Ms. Comer's."

"Okay, so I forgot. I will drive you there but can you get a ride home? I hate to drive after dark anyhow. And I am dead tired." It was an odd phrase considering she just came from her father's burial but I let it go.

So it was immediately settled. I could always walk the 3 miles home in a suit and white gloves. I was sure murderers would find me. Of course, Westport had no such crime but you would never know it from the way people acted. Everyone had a dog for protection and went around acting like someone was going to steal their stuff. I guess rich people act like that. They work really hard for their stuff and want to keep it all. I wouldn't really blame robbers and thieves for coming to Westport. There were a lot of people who had some really nice stuff. Our house wasn't one of them.

I was one of the last to arrive thanks to my

brother who had to get a ride to church first. We might be the only Irish in the entire country to be Protestants but sure enough, we belonged to the Saugatuck Congregational Church, one of the oldest in Connecticut. My brother belonged to the Pilgrim Fellowship which was really a bunch of dorks doing good stuff for others and then patting themselves on the back for doing it. Like, they visited old folks' homes and made sure they got their pictures taken for the newspaper. Really a bunch of phonies if you ask me. I wasn't really into helping other people much. I knew I should but most of the time they were really old and didn't really care if you helped them or not. One time my father and me went and emptied out an old guy's garage. We spent about 5 hours going to the dump and all. Did a pretty good job too and the old guy didn't even thank us. He was passed out on his hammock in the backyard. After that I was sort of into getting paid for what I did for others. Like my lawn service. Nobody expected me to do it for free. So they paid me and everybody was happy. I mean, ain't that the American way?

The boys sat on one side of the YMCA gym and the girls on the other. This was how we did it during each class. Some parents were there for the last class and all and Ms. Comer had decorated all the windows. It looked pretty silly because the gym was old and all but the ole lady wanted it to look classy, which was okay with me. She was about ninety years old and it was rumored she had been a Rockette at Radio City Music Hall. I wasn't sure what that was but Ms. Comer had always been nice to me, so what the hell? She always wore a formal gown with pearls around her neck. She also wore a lot of makeup which didn't fool anyone about her age. She was older than my grandfather that was for sure and he was dead!

I sat down next to Brian Hodges who had saved a seat.

"Where you been?"

"My grandfather died."

He looked at me like to see if I was kidding him or something. But even us goofballs didn't kid about someone dying.

"That sucks."

"He was pretty old."

"Listen, I think we are on about this steady thing again."

"What do you mean, on again?"

"Anne Daniels says she will go steady with Stevie and Betsy said yes to you. Olson already said yes to me so we are set."

"Betsy has a crush on you."

"She does?"

"That's what she told me at the graduation dance."

"Why didn't you tell me?"

"You've got enough girls already."

"You can never have enough girls." I hated Hodges when he acted like Kookie Burns and all. He was good looking but he wasn't that good looking.

"I don't want to," I finally said. Everybody had

arrived. I saw Betsy in one corner talking with Joannie.

"To go steady with Betsy? Are you crazy?"

"Not if she has a crush on you. I need for her to have a crush on me."

"I think girls are funny that way. They may want to go steady because all their friends on going steady."

"That's stupid!"

"So who said girls were smart?"

I pondered that question for a time. Maybe we were smarter than them. I never had thought that before. Girls always seemed to have the last say about everything, including the important word "no." And they were always getting better grades than us goofballs and most of the other guys too. So it never dawned on me that they might just be as dumb as us boys.

"Okay, I am in. You still got my ring?" I asked.

"Steve has all of them. He's going to hand them out."

"Hand them out? That ain't cool at all."

"We were going to do that last week at graduation."

"Well, that ain't how you are supposed to do it."

"How do you know how to do it? Oliver's sister is going steady and she told him that it was okay to arrange the going steady part of it. Then it was up to us to do the rest."

"What rest?"

"Give Betsy the ring and then go steady."

"I am not sure what going steady means."

"You can't go out with anyone else."

"We don't go out now anyhow."

"You want Betsy making out with all the other guys."

"No." I insisted.

"Then let's do it."

The place was packed to the rafters now. A ton of parents were there and Ms. Comer's waddled out to the middle of the "ballroom" and started talking about something. I couldn't hear a word she said. She had this high pitched voice. The very first class Hodges had worn a madras jacket and me a red blazer. This was okay for the first class but a suit was needed from then on. My father was so cheap he figured I could wait a week. Maybe save him some money. Anyhow, ole Ms. Comer didn't say anything but when we were leaving, she stopped both of us in our tracks.

"Now these are lovely jackets you boys are wearing," she said softly. "But you know the dress code for the class." Hodges didn't seem to mind but I felt embarrassed as hell. I guess she took me for one of those rotten kids who would one day rob banks for a living. Or murder people like on *The Twilight Zone*.

The first dance was a waltz. I was pretty good at the ole waltz. This was really formal dancing too. There was no hugging or anything. We also had dance cards. Pat Brenner was my first dance partner and she was much taller than me but pretty good looking. She had short straw-like hair and some huge blue eyes. She was cute in sort of a guy way but she was very smart too. Boys usually didn't like smart girls for some reason. I guess it made them feel dumber than they actually were. But since I was rethinking who was smarter, boys or girls, I walked over to Pat and bowed. I could be pretty aggressive at times. I really could. She stood and curtsied back and we started dancing.

"A lot of people here," I said trying to make conversation. With the waltz, you have to extend your arms way out and sort of go around in circles.

"My parents are here."

"Mine ain't, my grandfather just died." My way with girls was always to make them feel sorry for me. I am not sure where I learned this trick. Probably from some dumb movie. Pat ignored it anyhow.

"I hear you are going to go steady with Betsy?"

"Where did you hear that?" I asked dumbfounded.

"From Betsy."

"I guess that's good then." It was the best I could come up with.

"I think you are a real jerk and I told her to say no to you." She said out of the blue.

"Your eyes are too big," I responded. One thing you learn in Westport is to have a quick mouth. I could dish it pretty good if I really wanted to.

She stormed off as the dance ended.

I stood there like a statute. I looked over and saw Betsy staring at me. She smiled that cute smile and I smiled back. My best Alfred E. Newman imitation. She held up her ring finger and I saw my ring swinging on her middle finger.

I wasn't sure whether she was giving me the finger or showing me that we were now going steady.

Chapter 7

If you grew up in Westport, you NOT only had to learn to dance like a gentleman, but also to love Jesus. Unless of course you were Jewish. Not really sure how that works with them, but I guess Jesus is not their Boss. I started confirmation classes that Saturday at the Saugatuck Congregational Church. If you are wondering why a lot of things are named after Saugatuck in this town, so am I. The church was one of those old ones, all white with the big steeple on top. The kind of church George Washington would have gone to back then. Almost every 12 year old in Sunday school went to confirmation classes so you could become a member and take communion once a month. If you weren't confirmed you could not take the stale bread or wine (my brother told me it was grape juice) each month at Sunday services. I am not sure why that was a big deal but confirmation classes were a big deal. There were no grades but like everything in Westport you were being judged on whether you were a proper member or a heathen. There was no question I was going to hell as I have told you before but I still had to go to the classes. The crappiest thing about the classes was that they were held on Saturday mornings, which meant I had to get my butt out of bed early. It was also the day of a game and I needed my beauty rest, as my mother used to call it.

Mr. Oliver, Steve's father, was our confirmation teacher. He was an odd man in a cool sort of way. Tall, big features and one great tennis player. He could beat even the young kids and he was no spring chicken. He wasn't exactly your average teacher either. He told us that the answer to any question was "Jesus loves you." So, of course, us goofballs picked up on that with many questions.

"What does that passage in Genesis mean to you, Justin?" He would ask.

"Jesus loves you, sir," I would answer.

"Excellent. A+ answer," Mr. Oliver would answer.

The classes were supposed to get you ready to be a member of the church by teaching you about the history of religion. We didn't exactly pay too much attention to that kind of boring stuff and during the first class I got stabbed by Patty Taylor. It was an innocent enough stabbing if there is such a thing. Patty was sort of a guy-girl if you get my drift. She could probably beat the crap out of most of the boys in the class. She was a pretty good athlete too. Girls didn't play many sports but I saw Patty pop a fast ball into the woods behind Coleytown Elementary once. Her brother was pitching and she was killing the ball. Anyhow I was sort of bored as usual and started pretending that my pencil was a sword. I was slashing it around like Zorro. Patty was sitting next to me and we sort of started dueling. You know like Errol Flynn in Robin Hood dueling. Patty had the advantage because she had longer arms than me. So when I made a high dive she stabbed me right in the middle of my left hand. It wasn't a savage stab like on television but it did break the skin. The pencils were always sharp in church.

Of course I started crying like a baby. I admit I am not good with pain. And as I think back to my being hit in the balls by the baseball it might have been some kind of pain I was in that prevented me from fake running to first base. Mr. Oliver came running over like he was late for a tennis match. He looked at the wound and declared.

"You will be all right. Jesus loves you." He smiled. I didn't find it funny but the class did. They were laughing like it was the funniest thing in the world. Me, sitting there with a pencil stuck in my palm.

The wound was not bleeding bad or anything so they found me a band aid and I finished out the class. They didn't say a word to Patty Taylor who

I thought would get booted from confirmation class. Jesus couldn't love a stabber, could he?

Less optimistic, as usual, was my father.

"I think there is a piece of lead stuck in there, Justin. We got to get that out. You know what happened to Calvin Coolidge's son, don't you?" I didn't need a history lesson right now. But I did know who Coolidge was because we had to stop at his home in Vermont every stinking time we went up there. The place smelled like a barn and nothing was there but old furniture.

"He had a sore on his foot and wore socks that ran. The dye from the socks killed the kid." My father continued.

"Is that what is going to happen to me?" I bellowed. Now he had my attention.

"We need to get you to the doctor." My father proclaimed on his way out to catch his limo ride to the airport. "Your mother will take you to Dr. Beinfield's office. It is just down the road."

"Randolph, I hate doctors!" she yelled after

my father. The man in the grey flannel suit was gone.

Beinfield's office was just down Cross Highway. He had a big white house and an office on the side of the building. Even if you didn't have an appointment, ole Doc would take the wounded in at any time, day or night. He was a small man with a big nose and eye glasses dangling from one of those chains that stopped them from falling to the floor. I had been there many times and I liked the Doc. He always gave you a lollipop after he usually hurt the hell out of you while healing you.

The receptionist made us wait about a half an hour. My mother was smoking those Pall Malls like a chimney, one after another. I could tell the receptionist didn't much like smoke. She coughed a few times but my mother kept on puffing. My mother was sort of odd that way. She was really a pretty woman. She wore great clothes, all tailored and with pearls and all that makeup stuff. But sometimes she had sort of a chip on her shoulder.

She didn't take crap from anybody. Trust me, you didn't want to give her any either. But sometimes she could be sort of rude to people. Not like the rich assholes in town, but more like a snob from Vermont. You might not understand that but if you knew my mother you would.

"The doctor will see you now," the woman said standing and walking us into the small room with the couch-like operating table with paper on it. There always seemed to be an endless amount of paper on these tables. I wondered where they kept all the paper. I mean was there a roll somewhere underneath the cushion? I need to ask Doc Beinfield next time I get stabbed or something like that.

Ole Doc Beinfield walked in and stopped. He glanced down his chest for his glasses and found them dangling from the chain.

"Good day," he said. Ole Doc wasn't much for talking.

My mother said hello quietly and sat in the corner. She didn't like doctors. Like me, she wasn't much into pain. I hopped up on the table. I had been here before with a broken collarbone, a huge raspberry on my butt, a piece of glass in my ear and some kind of fungi on my leg.

"What have we done this time, Master Justin?" Doc said. I could tell he liked me because he started smiling when he looked at me. I had that effect on some people. Not many, but some. Doc Beinfield was also like Ole Man Wiggly in calling people "Master.' Old school guys.

"I got stabbed with a pencil by Patty Taylor, Doctor, sir."

"Well, that isn't very nice for a young lady to do, is it?"

"She ain't no lady," I replied. I heard a quiet sigh in the background from my mother.

The Doc was getting all his gear together after he looked at my hand. I took a quick look see at my mother who was looking very pale even for her and probably wishing she could light up a cigarette.

"You may feel a little prick now, Justin. I am going to numb the area before I go in."

"Go in, Doc?"

And then I heard a thud. My mother had passed out on the floor.

And I started bellowing at the top of my lungs.

Chapter 8

The 4th of July seemed to come quickly this year. With snow days we had gone to school late into June. I loved snow days but they came back to bite you in the long run. Like most good things there is a catch or something bad waiting for you ahead. The Marauders were undefeated, 6-0, and I was going steady with the adorable Betsy Firestone. I hadn't really seen her much after Ms. Comer's last dance. We didn't phone girls. That was considered sort of creepy. I didn't much like the phone anyhow considering everyone in the house could hear every word you said. I know girls liked to talk on the phone a lot. Joannie told me she spent hours on the phone with her buddies. Not sure what old Joannie talked about but she sure liked to talk. For boys though it was considered uncool.

May 30th and Memorial Day had come and gone but that was my father's favorite holiday. Us kids liked it too because we got to march through downtown Westport in the parade. I marched as a Little Leaguer this year but had also done so as a Cub Scout. They let just about everyone march in the parade, if they wanted. Even little kids were riding their bikes around. It was pretty cool actually. It was a day when the town sort of forgot it was a stuffy suburb and acted like the old farm town it used to be. The entire town of Westport turned out for the parade which went from the high school down Riverside Avenue across the river and through downtown. Folks would line up about two or three people deep watching and waving flags. It was real patriotic. They had the World War II guys marching and I gotta tell you, they looked pretty sharp. My father never did anything though. I guess he thought he was above all that kind of stuff. He didn't talk much about the war. I saw his uniform and he had a lot of medals and stuff all over the sleeves. I never asked him about it and he never offered anything about it either. I think some guys get pretty screwed up by wars. The ones who talk about it a lot were probably the ones cooking stew for the bases in New Jersey or something. My father wasn't the hero kind of guy though. He was more into being the ordering people around kind of guy, if you know what I mean.

My father liked Memorial Day because it was also his birthday. "Always give me a parade on my birthday," he used to say every year. And they did. He was real proud of that. Not sure why he thought that though. I mean nobody in the White House said "I think we should make Memorial Day on Randolph Hamilton Carmichael's birthday" or anything. But I guess you take what you can get sometimes.

July 4th was different. We had to put up the flag which was a major ordeal in the Carmichael household. It was a big flag and my father liked to hang it across our driveway. To do so, we had to use wire that went from one tree in the yard to my bedroom window. My father took care of the tree hookup with a ladder while I held the wire standing in my bedroom. My brother kept the flag from hitting the ground which was a big no-no to my father, the ex-military guy. Meanwhile my mother usually got lost somewhere on the other side of the house. She wasn't big on household stuff. She kept a pretty clean house according to my father but that was about it. She didn't rake or anything. I guess that was man's work.

"Pull it tight, Justin," my father yelled. "Duff, hold it up now. We wouldn't want the flag disgraced by touching the ground."

We did as we were told. Few questions were ever asked of my father. He was not really a commanding presence but people listened to him. Hodges once joked that he looked like the General in The Sgt. Bilko Show. A tad overweight with a big head and dominate features. He had once been skinny like my brother and me, but my mother's cooking had put on the pounds. I would probably end up like him as well. He was cheap to the point of embarrassment. My mother once called him "niggardly". My brother gasped at the word but my mother explained the true meaning of the word when my father was not present. It means being cheap if you are too lazy to look it up like I was. My mother told me or else I wouldn't have known either, so don't feel bad.

The flag flew gently in the breeze now completely parallel with the ground and perfectly level. "Tie it off," my father yelled looking over his shoulder from a hefty height on the ladder. As he did so, and I had a perfect view of him, his weight shifted from equally balanced on the ladder to his right. Normally this would not be a problem however he did it so quickly that it threw the ladder out of its nest on the pine tree and it, along with my father, began to fall. They say the heavier an object, the faster it will fall. My father must have weighed more than the ladder since he landed first. Hard!

My father was a screamer. I know this was genetic because I had inherited his genes and just as I would, my father screamed like a stuck pig when he hit the ground. He missed a rock by a foot but the ground was hard and my father soft. The ground won.

"Mom!" I yelled. "Dad's been hurt!"

Each year on July 4th the town of Westport packs Compo Beach with its residents to watch the fireworks. Compo is a pretty long beach and as you can imagine there were a lot of people there. It ain't the best beach around either. It is all rocky and you have to wear sneakers to get even close to the water otherwise your feet get all cut up and all. I liked the pool at Longshore much better than rocky old Compo. There were all sorts of jellyfish and garbage in the beach water too, which made things worse. The only time we really swam at Compo was when my father would come home all hot from the train ride and want a swim before dinner. It was a big deal and he would usually have to take the old Buick and put a horse blanket on the back seat for my brother and me to sit on. He didn't want to wreck the seats of the new Ford and all.

I have never particularly enjoyed fireworks. All that popping and banging with people screaming all over place. It seemed more like a war movie than fun but it was a family tradition and he never messed with those things. God forbid. My mother drove the station wagon that night despite her distaste for night driving since my father had broken his arm in two places when he fell off the ladder. His right arm lay on the open window sill in a white cast shining in the fading light. My father was quite mellow considering the pain he must have felt. It was a helluva lot worse than my stabbing or even my broken collarbone. You could see my father's bone sticking out before they put the cast on. It was really gross. My mother kept feeding him pills from a small brown container. By the time we hit the beach traffic my father was snoring away like my Uncle Arthur during his nap.

The beach as always was packed with cars, kids and a lot of dogs. Our dog, Dutchess, was a collie and a beautiful dog like Lassie. She once gave me a shiner right below the left eye. We were playing around and she jumped up right into my face. It hurt like hell and everyone at school thought I got into a fight with somebody but you couldn't get mad at this dog. She was too sweet and I don't say that about too many people or their animals. My father didn't let Dutchess in the house though. She shed too much hair, he said. Dogs are for outside. So poor Dutchess had a nice dog house and we didn't have dog hair in our house where my mother spent hours keeping it clean. Of course, Dutchess wasn't allowed in the car either. Matter of fact, Dutchess was kept on a long wire so she would not run away. I wondered why she would want to do that? But dogs were big in the suburbs.

You were often judged on the caliber or breed of your dog. If you had a mutt you were probably poor and if you had a show dog you were rich. I could never figure it out but people in the suburbs had rules. They weren't written anywhere but most knew them. In our home the furniture was more important than the dog.

My mother parked on the grass next to the basketball court. My brother immediately made a bee line for the court. Duff was a pretty good athlete for a creep. He could shoot hoops with the best of them. Meanwhile my mother had made dinner for all of us. She made fried chicken, potato salad and some canned baked beans. She spent a lot of time on stuff like that. She could really be thoughtful about us eating and all. I am not sure my father appreciated all she did because he thought he was some kind of hot shot businessman and all. Most fathers were like that with their wives in Westport. They went off to work and their wives took care of the house. I guess it wasn't too bad a way of life for women but it had to get old waiting on everyone all the time. My mother did a lot of other stuff too but she wasn't like most Moms who just stayed home and cooked. Maybe that is why she wasn't too hot a cook.

"You want something to eat, Randolph?" My mother asked.

"After my nap," he grunted with his head lying on the window frame.

My mother proceeded to set up a little table on the back of the station wagon. I was pretty hungry, so I helped her.

"You don't have to stay with me, you know." My mother said.

"I know but I don't know anybody." There was probably half my class somewhere on the beach but sometimes I didn't feel like hanging with the same kids all the time. Also I figured I might run into Betsy and what would I do then? I was beginning to think going steady may have not been such as great idea. I mean what was I suppose to do when I saw her? Kiss her like a mad man? Or just hug? It was very nerve wracking to tell you the truth.

"You take after me, Justin. You like your space." My mother said still putting out the food.

"It's hard here at this beach. Too many people." I replied. I sat next to the front tire with a piece of grass in my mouth.

"Some traditions are good. They are the core of our existence."

"Like Christmas Eve dinner?" I said. We had the same Irish meal every year. I hated all the food. My mother cooked the life out of the corned beef.

"Exactly. But this July 4th circus is for the birds," my mother said laughing. My Mom was pretty cool.

With the exception of my father, we all lay on the top of the Ford County Squire that night and watched the fireworks. Even my brother seemed to act normal for a change. My father slept through it all. I figured to myself that this was the last year

I was coming. Maybe in honor of my grandfather. It took us over two hours to get home with all the traffic. My mother was fit to be tied. My father slept through everything.

Chapter 9

Michael Babkie and I were the hellions of the neighborhood. We actually tossed logs down from our stone wall area onto cars passing by on Cross Highway. Then we would flee to the woods behind the Boyers' house next door. Nobody could find us. Why, you ask? I guess to get away with it. I could give you a list of stuff we did that summer and summers before that but you probably wouldn't believe half of it. We played Zorro and put a big "Z" on the Boyers' front porch. Since there were only three houses on the street, there was a limit to the number of victims.

The Boyers had two children: Pam and Stephen. Pam was a looker and we spent many nights attempting to get a peak of her naked from the woods that backed up to her big bedroom window. Since we once gave her a multi-colored pen to see her bare butt there wasn't much more to see. Mr. Boyer also had a collection of *Playboy* magazines in his bedroom closet. He had a stack about 20 deep, I would guess, and whenever the Boyers were gone Micheal and me would temp their rascal dog, Freddie, outside and then sneak in the back door of the house. We would snap up a couple of magazines and take off like thieves in the night. We were lucky we didn't get picked up by the cops.

One Halloween we got in some trouble with the police. Halloween was a big deal to Michael and me. I loved sugar and that night it was free. We mapped out where we would go in the busy well-populated neighborhoods. Since Gault Park was close by, we started there and then moved down Easton Road to another area packed with houses. Trouble was we also enjoyed Mischief Night the night before Halloween. That was traditionally when you broke stuff like mailboxes and threw eggs at car windows. Stuff like that. But this past year, it got way out of hand. Some big kids from high school did a job on some mail boxes and fences and the cops were called. Since Michael and I were well known in that area, we got called into the office at school. We both lied our asses off because we did do SOME damage but none of the big stuff. That is one thing about Michael, he was a better liar than me.

He met me one hot day in July on our gravel driveway. I was messing around with a golf club hitting a whiffle ball.

"Your father is gonna get mad at you if you chew up his grass," Micheal said.

"Yeah, you don't have to tell me that." The grass was more important than just about anything in our family.

"What you wanna do?" Michael asked.

"Not much."

"How about a game of baseball?" Michael asked. He was now in the prone position on my father's grass. We often played baseball in his backyard but we had been banned lately after Michael had hit a ball through his mother's kitchen window. The right field fence was the "Green Monster." His hit counted as a home run.

"Not enough guys around and your mother said no more baseball, remember?"

"She ain't home. Too hot anyhow."

"You wanna go over to Coleytown and see if we can steal some candy bars from the snack bar? Paul Kennedy said there was a hole in back of it. You can stick your whole arm through it."

Michael was up and heading home for his bike. We used to bike to school sometimes. It was probably about three miles but the roads were pretty good. My mother never seemed to mind and my father never knew. He would have surely stopped it since he was sort of scared about everything.

We were there in no time. Down Weston Road and then a right on Easton Road. The famous actor Paul Newman lived over by Coleytown and I used to go swimming at his pool after school with my good friend Timmy Wayne. His father was also as famous actor. Westport had a lot of famous guys like this but nobody much paid much attention to them. I mean it was no big deal swimming in the guy's pool because I didn't really know who he was, if you get my drift? Water is water after all. But a lot of hot shots had swimming pools. It was sort of a way of showing off. I mean how much time can you really swim in a pool during the cold weather of Connecticut?

"Can you get your hand through?" I asked Michael. He had climbed up on the little shed they had behind the hot dog stand at the baseball field. It was a pretty good place. We got hot dogs and cokes if we won a game which we did often as the Marauders. I felt sort of sorry for the guys who were on the losing teams. I guess they didn't eat.

"I think I got my arm stuck," Michael said.

"Why?"

"Because I can't get it out."

"What do you mean you can't get it out?"

"Ahhhh . . . duh. My arm is stuck in the hole."

If you knew Michael Babkie, you would laugh because he had arms skinnier than mine. They were like two sticks stuck to his body.

"What are we going to do?" He asked.

"Try harder."

"It is beginning to hurt. And hurt badly." And for the first time ever Michael Babkie began to cry or at least for the first time in front of me. He told me once he cried when his father smacked him one. But this was a first for me. It wasn't pretty. My father rarely spanked my brother or me but he had a better line to make you feel bad. He just said he was "disappointed" in you. Cruel as hell.

I climbed up the small shed. I was a pretty good climber.

"Here, let me try to pull," I said grabbing onto Michael's shoulder.

"Damn it, that hurts!"

"Try to relax your arm," I said. I wasn't sure exactly what that meant, but it sounded like something Doc Beinfield would say.

"Relax my arm? It's stuck in the damn hole!"

I paused for a second. He got his arm in there. It didn't get bigger and the hole didn't get smaller so something must be screwed up.

I started to pull on the arm some more when we both heard a loud yell. "Hey, you kids, get the hell off that shed!" I turned quickly to see a fireman in all his fireman stuff walking our way. The firehouse was right next to the school. I made one last pull on Michael's arm and sure enough it popped out and we fell backwards and flipped over on our way to the ground. We were pretty speedy kids when adults were around. And both of us were on our bikes and heading in the other direction towards the back of the school before the fireman got anywhere near us.

"We better go up North Avenue," I said.

"Good thinking, Justin. I don't want to go back anywhere near the firehouse."

"There are some pretty steep hills going up." I said. "You okay?"

"It will be fun going down Cross Highway," Michael said.

"Flying like a bird," I said standing up on my bike to get going.

There was another time when Michael and me decided to check out what a fallout shelter was all about. Fallout shelters were pretty big in Westport then because the rich families thought that even though the Russians might be bombing the hell out of New York City, they could escape being killed if they had a fallout shelter next to their house. Since they had a lot of money they could build it and stock it with food for about 10 years if they had to. It was pretty creepy thinking about it and all but the school would never let you forget it with all the hiding under the desks drills and then going down into the crummy basement of Bedford Elementary. And we did have a Nike site right there in town with a real live Army guy guarding it. No kidding. It was right down off North Avenue. Many parents wouldn't drive past it with their kids in the car for fear of scaring the bejeezus out of them.

So anyhow, Michael and me wanted to see a fallout shelter first hand. The only shelter I knew of was Joannie Olson's who lived pretty close by on Darbrook Road. Joannie's parents had a big house and a lot of money and Joannie didn't mind letting you know that her parents had a big house and a lot of money. She also let on they were putting in a fallout shelter that spring. I forgot all about it until Michael and me were sitting around that summer day with nothing to do. Again.

"You want to go over to Joannie Olson's house and see her fallout shelter?" I asked Michael.

"I am already there," he said going for his bike.

It only took about 10 minutes to bike over there. It was down North Compo Road and there were some hills there plus the old dump and the "Poor House". Westport actually had a house where poor people were put to live. It was sort of crummy too. I am not sure the people who lived there called it the "Poor House" but my mother sure did. She said it like it was some kind of disease too. My mother could be like that sometimes.

So we got to the Olson house and Michael rang the doorbell. One thing about Michael. He might have been shy around girls but not with adults. He would walk up to any person and speak his mind. He was not afraid of any teacher or principal or even a fireman. But he was scared of girls.

"Who is this?" Asked the woman who answered the door. She was a real looker and all dolled up in high heels and pearls around her neck. She was much better looking than Joannie who was covered with freckles.

"We are friends of Joannie, ma'am," Michael said.

"Oh, you mean Joan Annette?" She asked in a real phony kind of way. I hate parents who call their kid some fancy name when it's sort of obvious her name is really "Joannie."

"Yes, ma'am, we go to Bedford Elementary."

"Oh, and you are selling Cub Scout cookies?" She asked. Cub Scout cookies? I thought to myself this lady must be drunk.

"No, ma'am, we were wondering if Joannie . . . I mean Joan Annette was home."

"I am afraid not, young man. She has horseback riding lessons at the Hunt Club on Wednesdays."

"We really came to see your fallout shelter," I blurted out.

"Oh, aren't you two young men rascals. How did you know we have a fallout shelter?" She asked. "Oh, I guess Joan told you. Well, I guess it isn't a secret although I am sure we don't want everyone knowing, you know. They might stampede us if we do get bombed." She laughed to herself. She was seriously drunk.

"We get a Cub Scout badge if we can see one," Michael said. A total lie.

"Well, that makes a big difference than, doesn't it? Come right in now, boys. Don't mind the mess."

The house was sort of messy. There were

newspapers all over the place and cigarette butts. My mother would have started cleaning right up if she was there. I am glad she wasn't though. We walked through the kitchen with Michael leading the way. I saw him sort of checking Mrs. Olson out. She was a looker all right. I sort of wondered if Joannie would end up looking like her. But Mrs. Olson didn't have any freckles and I was sure freckles didn't just go away.

When we got to the garage there were these two big doors painted bright green.

"Here you go, boys. This is our fallout shelter."

Michael and I looked at each other.

"You have to open up the doors and then walk down. The shelter is underground, boys." Mrs. Olson said. I could smell her now. It was a mixture of perfume and liquor. I stopped looking at her so much.

Michael was opening up one door as I helped with the other. There was another door below that. It looked like a door to a bank vault. It was made out of metal and I began to think this might not be such a good idea. But Michael was on top of the steel door pulling on it before I could say anything. He really could be relentless once he got going.

"There you go, boys, see the ladder? You can just climb down there and take a quick look. My son Jeremy goes down there all the time. Please be quick though. I have a hair dresser appointment."

The ladder extended towards the floor below and Michael was down it faster than anything. I sort of stepped on to it very carefully. I didn't like heights and I didn't like ladders since my father fell off one on July4th. I heard Michael say "Holy Moly" and I made it a few more steps. The light was already on and the place was like an arcade of dirty pictures spread all over the place with magazines all on the floor. It was like in the back of Bill's Smoke Shop, except everything was all over the place. On the floor, on the small bed and on the card table down there. It was a regular porno shop.

"What is it, boys?" Mrs. Olson called out.

"Nothing, ma'am." Michael yelled back.

"I am coming down." She announced and as I looked up, I got a good view of up underneath Mrs. Olson's dress. I got sort of a sexy feeling all of a sudden.

"No, ma'am, we're done," Michael said.

And we were.

Chapter 10

The first time I jerked off was that summer.

It was the day after we visited Mrs. Olson's fallout shelter and I was feeling sort of sexy. If you are taking notes, this may have been my first time but hardly my last.

The make-out parties made me well aware of what having a boner was like. I wasn't real sure of the rest. I was up in my parents' bedroom looking out the window trying to see if Babkie was around. My father was in Venezuela or someplace important and my mother was playing golf at the Patterson Club. She was a great golfer for a woman. She was a great golfer for anybody. My brother was off at Boy Scout Camp for two weeks so I had the whole house to myself. I went up to the book shelves to see what sort of books they had. They weren't really dirty but some were pretty explicit on sex stuff and all. The kind of positions you have sex in and all. I guess adults need these kinds of guides. You would think they would know how to have sex but there are books on it and all. Trust me, there are. I really didn't know much, being a virgin and all. My only real experience was having a boner for about three hours at the make-out parties on a few Saturday evenings.

I was looking at this one book and it had pictures and all. Not really black and white pictures but sort of drawings. You could imagine all you wanted though. Nothing like the Olson fallout shelter library but not much was left to your imagination. They were pretty basic looking but I got this huge boner. I mean it was nearly busting through my pants. So I dropped my gym shorts and just had my underwear on. My boner was almost coming through the BVD's crotch. I dropped them too. Then I kept looking at the drawings in the book. I saw a pair of my mother's see-through underpants lying over on her chair next to the bed and I grabbed them and started to sort of drag them over my boner while I looked at the book. And then it happened!

I first thought I had to pee real bad and I got up to run to the bathroom but half way there I just exploded. This white stuff just fired out of my dick all over the place. It hit the mirror on the vanity and sprayed the door to the bathroom. It was like an explosion of white foam all over. At first it scared the hell out of me. I thought it was some sort of disease or something. I really did. And then everything felt really good. It felt like part of my insides had just escaped. It is sort of weird to explain but I was really relaxed. Like I could take a nap.

Then I heard someone knocking on the door. I panicked. I started to clean up the mess like a madman. There was white junk all over the mirror and the bathroom door. It was like everywhere. It made the towel all sticky and I noticed my mother's underwear had taken a hit as well. I quickly put the book back and got dressed. I looked from their window and saw it was Michael Babkie standing in the driveway. He saw me peeking at him.

"Hey, Justin, what are you doing up there? I've been down here for about five minutes." A total lie but Michael lied all the time.

"What do you want?"

"What do you mean what do I want? Come on out. We will go do something."

"Okay, I will be right down."

I wadded up my mother's underwear and the towel. I thought about putting them in the hamper in the bathroom but I knew my mother would notice them there. I made them into a smaller wad and stuffed them in my shorts' pocket. I still had sort of a boner so I had to wait a while longer before I saw Michael. I gave it a good pinch but that didn't seem to help either. I actually felt like I was getting all sexy again. I went down to the kitchen and got some ice from the freezer and put it down my pants. That did the trick. I went quickly soft although I had a wet stain in my crotch.

I decided desperate situations required desperate measures. I walked through the den and out the door in a super hurry.

"I gotta go, Michael. See ya." I took off for the woods hoping he would not follow me. No such luck.

"Hey, slow down. What's that you got in your pocket?"

There are just so many things you can share with your buddies. You can talk all you want about sports or your parents or even girls but not jerking off. I knew there had to be a rule against that. I can run like a rabbit and I knew Michael would give up. He was sort of used to people blowing him off and he usually took it well, I must say that for him.

When I was sure he was not following me, I decided to bury the towel and panties. I was pretty sure my mother had more than one pair and we had a ton of towels. I thought about burning them but I tried that once before. When my parents were gone and I was staying with the Boyers,

I stole some of Mr. Boyer's *Playboys* and did a quick survey of them back at my house. I figured there was no safe place to hide them because my mother was like a hawk with any of my stuff. She was probably looking for cigarettes and maybe even drugs. Not that I knew anything about that. So I started a fire out by where my father burned leaves. Trouble was the wind started blowing really hard and the flames started flying around. Pretty soon I nearly had a brush fire going in our woods. Nude pictures were flying around like sparks. I finally got the hose and put it out but it was a close call. My father wanted to know all about the burned area but I sort of lied and he got busy with something else. He was like that.

So I found a soft area down by the creek and started digging away with a stick. I got a pretty deep hole going. I was good with my hands. I planted stuff in the garden all the time. And so I buried the evidence. I put leaves all around it so nobody would think anything about it. I climbed back up the hill to our grassy area and saw my mother pull into our circular driveway. She never liked to put the car in the garage for fear of taking off half the side of the house. So she left the car out when my father was gone. She saw me right off and waved, a cigarette hanging from her mouth.

"Hey, did you win?" I asked, sort of skipping in a joyful mood.

"What is that on your shorts?" She asked.

Chapter 11

My mother was very Republican. She was also very political. My father could care less unless the government was messing with his company or business. They both liked Ike, President Eisenhower, that is. My father sometimes used to joke: "The Eisenhower doll. Wind him up and he doesn't do anything for 8 years." My father was like that. Nothing much made him happy. But the joke didn't make my mother happy.

My mother was the only daughter of a State Senator from Vermont. That was my recently dead grandfather. So on the third Tuesday in July while my brother remained hidden at Boy Scout camp I was yanked down to Republican headquarters next to Gold's Deli to learn all about elections. I must say that some of the history classes in elementary school did interest me some. More than those stupid math and science classes! So to make my Mom happy, I got out of bed pretty early for me and went with her to work for Richard Nixon for President.

"Mom, I have licked about a thousand envelopes. My mouth is so dry," I whined as we sat in Nixon headquarters in Compo Shopping Center off the Post Road. It was like noon and the place was pretty slow. We had been there since about 9:00 a.m. and it felt like I had been licking envelopes for 8 hours. I was being sort of nice to my mother these days since I ruined her underwear and then buried it. She never found out.

"Why Nixon?" I asked.

"He is a Republican."

"What does that mean?"

"He will do right by this country."

"I sort of like Kennedy."

"He's Catholic."

"So was Dad."

"Not anymore," she said angrily. "We don't want our President taking orders from the Pope."

"Why would he do that?"

"That is what Catholics do. They swear allegiance to the Pope."

"What does the Pope do?"

"Ask your father," was her harsh reply and I knew better than to pursue any more questions.

My mother spent most of her time at Nixon headquarters on the phone talking with voters or talking with other women. Not many men were there and I was the only jerk licking envelopes on a great summer day in Westport. I might have been the only kid in the whole country working for Richard Nixon.

"Mom, my mouth is all stuck together," I said, whining again.

"Finish that pile there and we can go. It is important."

"What am I sending out?"

"It is a flyer reminding people to vote."

"Vote for Nixon?"

"To vote Republican."

"I am not sure I like Nixon. He looks sort of creepy to me."

"He is the Vice-President of the United States, I will have you know."

"His eyes look like he is dishonest."

"How can you say such a thing?" My mother stood over me like one of my teachers.

"I just like Kennedy's looks better."

"Well, looks are NOT all that counts."

"Tell that to the 6th grade girls."

"Are you having trouble at school, Justin?"

"We are on summer break, Mom."

"No, but I mean really. Girls can be funny at your age. One day they like someonc and the next they don't. And if I remember correctly, they are not always nice about it."

"Were you, Mom?"

"What?"

"Nice to the boys."

"I used to try to beat them at everything they thought they were better at than me."

"Did you win?"

"Ask your father. Now get those envelopes finished and I will take you to the Crest Drive-In for lunch."

"Can we hit some golf balls afterwards?"

"We'll see. But you must finish those envelopes."

"Why?"

"Oh, Justin, you ask too many questions."

So I finished the envelopes and hoped Kennedy would win. I kept staring up at the picture of Richard Nixon. He seemed to be staring back and saying, what kind of sap are you sitting there looking at me? I looked at the brochure I had been sticking in envelopes for close to five hours. It had a sleazy picture of Nixon on the right top corner and then it said "Why America Needs Richard Nixon." It really wasn't a question but it did list a whole lot of stuff about Nixon. Like under "We need a President who knows the job," it said that Nixon was Vice-President and all. I guess he was saying Kennedy didn't know much. Then it said "We need a President who knows other nations." My father knew a lot about other countries and he told me once they threw garbage at Nixon in Venezuela. He was sort of laughing at it until my mother gave him the ole evil eye. Then it said "We need a President able to lead America and the free world." They used a lot of free world stuff in school. I guess they were talking about the Commies in Russia and all. It was sort of scary to a kid my age to think the commies might blow the whole damn world up some day. But I had my own theory. I didn't think the Commie people really wanted to take over the world. From where I stood it looked like they lived a pretty crummy life over in Russia and they really just wanted to live like Americans. I don't know if it was true or not but that is what I believed. This hiding under the desks and going to the basement of Bedford Elementary was pretty stupid. I bet the Commie kids didn't have to do that kind of stuff.

The more I read about this guy Nixon, the more I didn't like him. On the bottom of the brochure it said "With your support, Dick Nixon will win again in 1960." I never did like the name Dick. Every Dick I knew was a real dickhead. I mean it. There was this guy in our Coleytown class named Dick Hurtz and everybody made fun of his name. But it wasn't his name that made him a creep. He was a jerk, a total creep with or without the funny name. He could have been Dick Johnson and he would have been the same jerky creep.

As I munched on my Crest hamburger, mayo but hold the pickles with lettuce and tomato, I asked my mother why she liked Nixon.

"I really don't like him that much," she answered. She was smoking a cigarette and sipping on an ice coffee. She loved ice coffee. Perhaps she was the only person in the town who drank it.

"Then why are we working for him?"

"I wouldn't call what we did 'work', but I do

like Cabot Lodge. He is Vice-President Nixon's running mate."

"Why doesn't Lodge run for President?" I asked. Normally I would just sling along a bunch of question to pass the time or to be sort of phony like I was interested and all but this stuff, politics, did interest me.

"That is the way of politics. Nixon won the primaries and got the nomination of the party."

"Why do they call them parties?"

"Justin, you ask too many questions." She took a big whiff of the cigarette and downed the ice coffee. The waitress who came out to the car from the kitchen drive-in place took our stuff and gave me a wink.

My mother saw her and said, "No wonder you like Kennedy."

After our lunch I had a dental appointment. I went to this guy in Weston called Dr. Ayers. He was a good looking guy with a good looking wife and he had his office in his house. I gotta tell you, I will hate this dentist forever. I had to go every six months but it felt more like every month I was going because I had a lot of cavities. I guess it came from all the sugar I ate. My Mom couldn't cook good but she could bake some great stuff. So we had brownies, chocolate cookies or cake nearly every night. It was one reason my father was fat and I was always getting my teeth fixed. Sugar ain't good for your teeth, you know.

Doc Ayers was one of those guys who didn't smile much. He was so good looking he probably felt he didn't need to be nice for people to like him. There were a lot of those guys in Westport. Most good looking guys are real successful but not too friendly. I found this to be true anyway. One thing about going to ole Doc Ayers was that it hurt like hell. He didn't use any novocaine or anything to stop pain. He started off with this grinding drill which hurt like all hell. Doc Ayers would tell me to lift my right arm but he was usually leaning against it so I couldn't lift it even if I wanted. I was a pretty good patient though. A lot of kids would yell and scream but I just sat there and took the pain for all the sugar I ate to wreck my teeth.

Once Doc Ayers was done with the grinder, he would start packing the hole with his hammer like tool. The pain was pretty much gone by then. He sometimes would squirt a bunch of air in there and that was like sticking a dagger in your brain and up your butt. Wow, did that hurt! Then the ole Doc would use this real fast sounding drill that pounded down all the filling stuff. I could relax by then. It usually took about 30 minutes. I gotta tell you, being a dentist must be a tough way to make a living, spending your whole day looking and sticking your hands into someone else's mouth. But I guess for ole Doc Ayers, it must have been nice working out of your home with your good looking wife as your receptionist. Must have been even better than going to New York City every day on a train.

The Doc would always give me the lecture about brushing my teeth better after every visit and my mother would frown when he told her I had a couple more cavities. Then they would give me a lollipop for being a survivor of all the pain and all. Of course when I my father heard, he would always get sore about how much money it cost to pay Doc Ayers.

It was pretty much routine going to Doc Ayers. It hurt like hell though so he probably enjoyed hurting people. Don't let anybody try to fool you about that.

Chapter 12

We remained undefeated through 7 games. I was batting .312 and feeling pretty good about myself. We played the Cubs that Thursday. And that meant Murray Rosen who was a very good pitcher. The Cubs were a pretty good team and in second place. So it was a big game for us.

I led off with a single to left field. Murray threw me a big fat curve ball on the inside of the plate and I smacked it right by the third baseman's glove. I knew Murray from school. He was sort of a quiet guy whose migraine headaches got him out of school a lot. I didn't really know him well enough to ask him whether he was faking or not but I figured it was pretty cool that he got to go home. I knew this gal at Coleytown Elementary, Peggy Conner, who told our teacher she got so nervous before a test she would get sick. So they didn't make her take any tests! I thought it was a great idea. I tried it once and Mrs. Wolfson sent me to the principal.

Murray looked over at me and gave me sort of a strange look. He had deep seated eyes sort of spooky like and so I looked the other way. Brian Hodges was next up and Murray hit him on the first pitch. Swear to God. He hit him right on the hip. Brian winced, but he was a tough little guy and trotted to first base. Mike Stephenson, a lefty, was up next. On the first pitch, he hit a towering drive that went straight over my head and over the center field scoreboard. Home run! I started trotting around third base slowly sort of pretending like I was Mickey Mantle. I looked over at Murray. He had this look in his eyes and he was staring right at me like he was staring right through me. It was creeping me out but this time I kept staring back at him. I had never been in a real fight, as I told you before but that didn't mean I couldn't or wouldn't fight. Usually it involved my brother who had a knack for teeing people off. I would usually try to help him and I usually bit the hell out of the other guy with my two big front teeth. They were monsters. So I guess I knew how to fight. Even though I was scared of most things I wasn't afraid of Murray Rosen.

When I touched home plate is when it all started to happen. Murray started charging at me screaming at the top of his lungs. I couldn't make out exactly what he was saying but it was in such a tone that it didn't matter much. He reached me as I turned to my left from home plate. Murray was not a big guy but I was pretty tiny. He hit me in the stomach head on and we both went plowing into the Cubs' catcher. I don't know the catcher's name but he was a big guy. We ended up in a heap at the umpire's feet. The ump was a local Westport cop. Most of the umps were cops and we got to know them pretty well. This cop was named Larry. He was skinny with big arms. The kind of guy who might carry a knife if you know what I mean.

Murray was still screaming something when Officer Larry pulled him off me. The catcher went off to the side and started crying. I am not sure why guys cry when they do. Girls can cry at any time. You make fun of their new bra or something like that and they cry pretty quickly. But boys are sort of different. Sometimes a boy will just start crying for no reason at all. And that is what the catcher did. Officer Larry took Murray in his left arm and just held him up by the collar of his uniform. He was a strong bastard, I will give him that. Lousy teeth though. I took off like a bat out of hell for the dugout and safety. But nobody was in the dugout. Everybody was out in the field fighting with someone on the opposite team. It was like a free for all in professional wrestling if you can believe that stuff's for real. This was real.

In the midst of the fight a band of protesters paraded down the paved playground behind Coleytown Elementary toward the ball field. I watched them from the corner of the dugout. I was not about to bite my way out this wild fight. They held the same signs as they had at Longshore: "Save Cockenoe Island." There were at least 100 of them this time around. They wore an assortment of attire from a three piece suit to a clown like Hawaiian shirt and sandals. Many were fat old ladies with smock dresses like in art class. They walked single file in silence. When they turned the corner by the right field fence closest to the home field bleachers the fighting stopped. There was near silence except for a few players crying from their wounds. Even Murray Rosen who was being held in the corner of the backstop fence by Officer Larry had quieted. The protest stopped all the fighting and kept everyone quiet.

They strolled down the bleachers and a few people stood and clapped. But there was little support. Most of the spectators just looked at this group of odd balls that had shut everybody up. At the entrance to the field by the Cubs' dugout, they swung their long line onto the field and crossed the middle of it. No umpire tried to stop them. Everyone got out of their way. The some odd 100 people marched by second base and into the outfield. Even though they looked pretty ragged, they marched in perfect cadence. At the end of the field in front of the centerfield scoreboard they veered right and then left as half the marchers went to left field, the other to right field and the school. They finally reached their final stop in perfect formation by the outfield fence. It was like the cadets at the Army-Navy game.

By now nearly every kid had returned to his team's dugout. We all sat quietly many with bruises and already swelling eyes staring at the protesters. But no sooner had the line formed its final column when another line of protestors come from behind the Marauders' dugout. Behind us were a small set of bleachers and behind that was a row of bushes. A bunch of houses were behind the bushes. And this is where the next formation came from. They were sort of sloppy in dress too but their signs were really something. One read: "Get the Nukes out of Westport" in bold white letters on a background of Columbia blue. I expected to see a sign for Nixon but there wasn't one. A few celebrities were in this rank and file. Paul Newman, Joanne Woodward, Kirk Douglas and a few I didn't recognize but you could tell they were real important hot shots.

They paraded through the exit gate by our dugout and again, half went left along the third base line and the other half right along the first base line. When it was all done the entire field was assembled with protestors, signs and a perfect ring around the entire baseball field. It was pretty cool. It really was. The only thing that got me was they didn't do anything. They just stood there.

We won the game by forfeit.

Chapter 13

My father always wanted a swimming pool in the backyard. My mother wouldn't let him have one.

"We live 5 miles from Long Island Sound, we don't need a pool. Pools are only for rich people," she said and meant it. It also meant we were not going to get one.

Two days after the historic riot-protest game which made the New York newspapers I was invited to Buddy Scully's birthday party. The Scullys must have been rich because it was a pool party. Max Scully was an author in a town full of writers. His son was sort of a goofball and, according to my mother, the New York Times crossword puzzle champion. Max was sort of a nutcase too.

The entire crowd was there including Betsy and I waved to her as I got out of the station wagon. My father had almost taken me over in the Buick, the deteriorated "station car", which was a sure sign of poverty but at the last moment I talked him out it. I was going steady with Betsy. She had my ring and had agreed to the arrangement. This was via messenger but still "yes" meant "yes" even if I was still not sure what steady really meant. Did it mean we only could talk to one another? Was I the only boy she could talk to? Or was it like a Chinese-type relationship which my father had told me about where we only made out at make-out parties or danced at the dances? I needed to know some of this stuff but I didn't know anybody I could ask. Certainly not my parents and my brother, forget it. I was certain however that answers would not come from Betsy herself. She was as shy as me.

"Hey, Justin," Brian Hodges said, approaching. "Hell of a game yesterday, hey?"

For some reason Hodges had acquired the habit of saying "hey" a lot lately. Sort of like the Canadians in Vermont.

"We won, that's what counts," I countered with my best Yankee Bobby Richardson impersonation.

"Yeah, right. Hey, did you hear that Murray got sent to the funny farm?"

"You mean Hallbrook?" I asked. Hallbrook was the hospital off Long Lots Road where they sent retards. It was the subject of many jokes. Not so funny to me now. Westport also had another one down by the Post Road. It was more some sort of sanitarium or something like that. I think if you got some kind of contagious disease, they sent you to that place.

"Sure thing. My mother heard it from Murray's neighbor. Probably practicing up on his golf game, hey?" Hallbrook had a 3 hole golf course on its big front lawn. The standard joke was to ask if your mother stopped by for a round of golf at Hallbrook when she was late picking you up. I used to tell that joke a lot. Joke's on me now.

"Brian, forget about Murray. Tell me about this steady thing. What are you doing with Olson."

"She hasn't talked to me yet."

"I thought you were going steady."

"Hey, I am just waiting for her to come to me."

"That might be a long wait knowing Joannie."

"Hey, they all come around."

We stood by the pool. There was a ton of kids. Buddy knew everyone and I guess everyone liked him. My mother got him a dumb gift, a puzzle game, so my days were numbered with him. Dumb or cheap gifts were a friend breaker. Junior High would be different anyhow. Buddy was a terrible athlete and in 7th grade sports started to separate the men from the boys. At least my brother believed that and he could play hoops. So I guess the dumb gift had to do.

I wasn't sure what to do next. I was not wild about stripping down to my bathing suit. I wore one of my father's Harvard shirts to cover my puny body. I was sort of a slob at heart to tell you the truth but in this case the shirt served its purpose. I really didn't want to show my 86 pound weakling body to Betsy so I just stood looking at the kids in the pool. Of course, she had seen me clutching my nuts in the baseball game so my puny body couldn't be that bad.

A short man with wild hair approached us from the house which was set above the pool. The Scullys were loaded. Their house was twice the size of my house. The pool was about the size of my house! Mr. Scully wore a floppy hat and I recognized him as Max, the writer and also a protestor from the day before. His face was almost burned red like a bad sunburn while his legs were white. For a rich guy he sort of looked funny looking. But Mr. Scully was the kind of man who really didn't care much about what anybody thought about him. You could tell by the way he dressed and the way he moved around. He was sort of cool being uncool at the same time.

"Attention, children! Attention!" Mr. Scully cried out. Nobody much paid him too much attention. I did though.

"I said ATTENTION," he yelled. And then everybody was quiet. During this time I very quickly took off the Harvard shirt and dove into the pool. My head came up from the water just as Mr. Scully continued.

"Listen very carefully," he said in a lower and calmer tone. "If any of you kids pees in this pool, it will turn red." There was a low murmur among us kids. "That's right," he continued. "If any one of you takes a leak, the water will turn red." He gave a big clap of his hands and bowed slightly in thanks and returned to the house. Little did he know we all had heard this before many times. We were not dumb little kids from the sticks. This was Westport, after all. The Longshore lifeguard told us this every afternoon, the entire summer, each day and every hour. There was a slight snicker among us kids but everyone resumed their activities. Most of us kids in Westport grew up pretty quick and realized the games parents play. We were on to their tricks.

I was a pretty good swimmer. I had learned in

Cub Scout camp up at Candlewood Lake. Unlike being up at bat, I was not afraid of the water but I didn't much like the ocean or Long Island Sound. My father told me once there had been a shark sighting off the unpatrolled portion of Compo Beach. I never swam there and didn't really enjoy the beach anyhow. I liked the pool. I swam at the YMCA pool which was stocked full of piss and too much chlorine to fight it. The chlorine was so strong that your eyes would tear up after you got out. The pool at Longshore was much better but it was a salt water pool and stung your eyes too. I liked the Scully-type pool, if you must know. It probably sounds sort of snobby coming from a goofball like me but give me good ole clear water with just a tiny hint of chlorine. That is until it turned red.

"Everybody out," some kid yelled. "Someone peed in the pool. It is turning red." And sure enough the water coming from the pump on the side of the pool was as red as Joannie Olson's hair.

There was a mass exit. The girls of course were screaming for some unknown reason. Considering where their pee came from, it was a wonder many didn't have permanent pee stains around their privates. But then how did I know. As least us boys had a faucet!

"I think it was Justin," yelled Quincy Smollin. Smollin was a jackass we all knew from church and Saugatuck Elementary. He was a butter ball and a lousy athlete. He was always smoking behind the snack bar at games and he thought he was pretty cool. I knew he would be a "greaser" and work on cars all his life.

"Up yours," I yelled back and I saw Betsy turn away. Damn Quincy. Now everyone was staring at me.

Then ole Mr. Scully came down the stairs from his house. He was laughing so hard I thought he was going to fall over. He laughed like a jerk really. One of those guys who slaps people on the back when they think something is funny. I didn't think it was funny because I figured him out right off. He was putting red dye in the pool to fool us kids. And now I was getting pointed out by Quincy Smollin for doing it.

"It's safe," Mr. Scully was saying while he continued to laugh. "It is only red dye, I hope nobody really peed in the pool but it was all a joke." I looked over at Buddy Scully and he wasn't laughing. He wasn't even smiling. Some of the real kiss up guys and girls were smiling. I was just staring at Quincy with a dirty look. Quincy was looking the other way. He had played his hand and lost. Now it was all out war. You don't accuse someone of peeing in the pool and then back down.

So I wandered over to Quincy. Brian Hodges was at my back and a few other guys. I wished Dale Hopkins was there but he wasn't invited. Dale would have punched out Quincy faster than Superman. But I wasn't Dale.

"Why are you telling everyone I peed in the pool, you jerk," I said, acting like I was some kind of tough guy.

"Oh, bug off, Justin. I could smash you to bits in one second."

"Just try," Brian said from behind. "Justin has friends." Hodges stood behind me. Alone now.

"I don't need any friends to kick your butt, Smollin", I said bravely. It was a fact I had never been in a fight. As I told you, I helped my brother out sometimes by biting the hell out of the other guy. But one on one, it would be my first. "You think you are so cool cuz you are going steady with Betsy Firestone," Smollin said. There was a bunch of kids behind him now.

"Yeah, well, I also play for the Marauders," I replied. I am not sure why I said this but I did. I guess I thought it was cool.

"Little League is for jerks," Smollin said and a bunch of kids laughed. Then from my right side came Brian with a running block on Quincy. He rammed Quincy right in his fat belly and was on top of him slugging like mad. It wasn't until Mr. Scully came running did Brian stop. I was very proud of my buddy. I slapped his back when he flew out of Mr. Scully's grasp.

"Fight your own fights from now on, Justin," Brian said.

I looked at him like I hardly knew him. He just walked away. Hodges could be sort of funny at times. I knew him from Little League at first and then went to Bedford Elementary with him for 6th grade. We did everything together along with Steve Oliver. We played sports and walked downtown. We formed a fraternity together. We were like the "Three Musketeers". But Brian could be sort of moody. He would never call me up or invite me over to his house. I think he lived in sort of a crummy house off South Compo. We both hung around at Oliver's house where they had 7 kids and about 10 dogs. It was a fun place to be. Steve and me were never in competition but I think Brian sort of was with me and, I guess, me with him. I could always feel that when I was around him.

Chapter 14

The phone rang again in the middle of dinner. And once again, it was the same thing all over again.

"Who could that be?" My father asked.

"Why doesn't someone answer it and find out," my mother suggested as she puffed on a Pall Mall.

"I will get it," my brother offered. He was fresh back from Boy Scout camp and a real brown nosing do-gooder.

"Carmicheal residence, this is Duff. May I help you?" We all were listening.

"Yes, ma'am. Just a minute please."

The stomping of my brother's combat boots could be heard. He had become a military GI Joe at camp.

"It is for you, Mom," he announced.

"Take a message," she said.

"It is Mrs. McCarthy."

"Oh," my mother said, putting out her cigarette and rising from her chair.

"What does she want?" My father asked.

"Apparently, she wants to talk to me, Randolph," she replied. My father looked at both my brother and me and rolled his eyes.

My mother often talked on the phone and she wanted privacy when she did. Since my father was too cheap to get an extension, she got an extra long cord for the kitchen telephone and dragged it upstairs. No one else did so. At least no one else tried to. I sometimes I went into the hall closet.

After we all had finished our dinner and it was my brother's turn to clean the table which he did without complaint, my mother returned.

"What did she want?" My father asked again.

"She wants to take Justin to the All-Star game at Yankee Stadium."

"What . . . "? My brother yelped.

Tommy McCarthy was not a good friend but he

was a Marauder. That meant something at least to me and I guess to him. Mrs. McCarthy was a real looker. She had super long blond hair and wore glasses to drive. I didn't really check out her body and all considering she was Tommy's mother and all. But she was okay. I had seen her at games. She used to keep score of all our games.

We drove into Yankee Stadium. This was a first for me because we usually took the train with my father. My Dad would take my brother and me to one Yankee-Red Sox game a year. He got real hot shot seats and all being that he was a big wig at U.S. Rubber and all. All big shots sat in the box seats while the sort of slob guys sat in the bleachers. That sounds sort of snobby but that is the kind of thing you notice when you grow up in Westport. Sometimes I wished I was sitting in the bleachers.

I loved the All-Star games. This was the second year they played two games. The National League had already won the game two days before in Kansas City. Here at Yankee Stadium though I figured they were a sure bet to win big time. They had a lot of Yankees on the starting team: Mantle, Maris, Moose Skowron and Yogi with Whitey Ford as starting pitcher. Since I was a big Yankee fan, it was like a dream come true watching them play in Yankee Stadium. It was really something, I gotta tell you.

The seats were real good. I guess the McCarthys were rich too. They had a bunch of kids so I was feeling really special coming along to the game. Tommy was a big Yankee fan too so we cheered as loud as we could during batting practice. We made so much noise that Mickey even looked over and smiled.

The game was sort of disappointing. It was Willie Mays' return to New York after the Giants moved to San Francisco and he didn't disappoint any of his fans. He hit a home run in the second inning as did Hank Aaron and it was quickly 2-0. Vernon Law was pitching for the National League and nobody seemed to be able to hit him. The more we yelled, the worse it got. The National League got another run in the 3rd and one in the 7th. The American League could hardly get a base runner. Tommy and I were both sort of down about the game and stopped yelling so much.

"We could leave early, boys," Mrs. McCarthy said. She was scoring the game in her big score-book. My grandfather had taught me how to score with the numbers and all. I was the kind of kid who liked to play more than watch and keep score. My brother was the score keeper kind. Before the game I had bought him and me signed autographed baseballs from both leagues. They were 5 bucks a piece. I sort of doubted whether they were real autographs. They looked sort of printed on and 10 bucks was a lot of money to me. That was about 15 lawns to mow. But I guessed my brother would like it. He would like the American League ball since he was a big Red Sox fan. Sometimes I could be a thoughtful kid. I really could. But there was a limit with my brother.

"We want to stay to the end, Mom," Tommy pleaded. Good ole Tommy was a good egg. He was that. I never noticed him much but we were sort of alike. He had some serious buck teeth and ragged hair which made us similar in that way. He was bigger than me too. But I could play short stop better than he ever could.

The Nationals scored 2 more runs in the 9th inning. I was really down now and ready to leave. Mrs. McCarthy was still keeping score. She seemed to be more interested in doing that than watching the actual game. She didn't miss a pitch though in scoring it. What was missing was Tommy. He vanished after the first run in the top of the 9th. Now the game was nearly over with 2 outs in the bottom of the American League's 9th and no Tommy.

"Do you know where Tommy is?" I asked his mother.

"Oh, he always does this. He vanishes at the end of every game we go to. It is very upsetting."

There were still a lot of fans left in the stadium. I guess they wanted to make sure they got every last look at some of the greatest players of all time. When the final play was done by striking out Yogi on three pitches, Mrs. McCarthy closed up her score book and put it in her oversized beach bag. She was sort of a cool woman for someone old enough to be my mother.

"Still no Tommy," I said.

"Yeah, he will come back."

"When?"

"When he is good and ready." Mrs. McCarthy leaned down and grabbed a book out of her bag and began reading.

"Why does he do this?" I asked. There was a seat in between us and I sort of leaned over.

"He is like his father. Stubborn and Irish."

"I guess that means you are for Kennedy?" I tried to make conversation. I honestly liked Mrs. McCarthy and she had taken me to an All-Star game, after all. I don't normally talk to adults much. I find them pretty boring and usually they don't like to talk to me much except maybe my mother but I guess she has to.

"Of course," she answered. "I am in love with JFK."

"Seriously? Have you met him."

"I have met him. Once. And I fell madly in love with him the moment I laid eyes on him." Mrs. McCarthy was very animated with her hands when she talked. She always looked you straight in the eye when she spoke to you. I thought it was a neat habit.

"Where did you meet him?"

"Oh, that is a long story and we must be going," she said. "Here comes Tommy. Right on time."

"My mother is for Nixon." I blurted out. "I don't think she has met him."

Mrs. McCarthy pulled back her long blond hair and laughed. She was beautiful. "Tell your mother Nixon is a crook."

Chapter 15

Freddy English called the next day. Early. My mother woke me up to tell me that he called.

"He wants you to call him."

"Mom, it is too early."

"The early bird gets the worm." She said, a Pall Mall hanging from the right side of her mouth.

Freddy lived over by downtown. Us kids spent a lot of time at the YMCA downtown after school when school was in session. But when it wasn't, nobody seemed to go down there. The movie theater was an old dump and even though Thompson's Pharmacy had the best fries in the world it was long ways from my house to downtown. I knew my mother wouldn't drive me. She was really into the Nixon campaign now and every spare moment was spent on the phone calling to gain support for the crook. I didn't tell her, by the way, what

Mrs. McCarthy had said about the Vice-President. It would have made my mother mad and nobody wanted my mother mad at them, including me.

Freddy also lived up by the Fine Artist School where the guy from *The Twilight Zone* worked. That show scared the beejeezus out of me. There was no way I was going to walk by there. Like the house behind the Crest Drive-In all us kids thought the place was haunted. I don't even like to think about those episodes on *The Twilight Zone* when the man loses his head in his sleep. Don't even think about it! The scariest stuff on television and I won't even watch. My mother won't let me watch. My father doesn't watch television,but he wouldn't let me watch either. And all of it was coming out of that school by the river by Freddy English's house, which, by the way, was across the street from a cemetery!

Freddy's parents didn't actually own the house. They rented it and this was a sure sign of poverty in Westport. I only know because my mother used to bring our laundry to Freddy's house to be ironed. The Englishs were survivors of the Holocaust. That is where the Germans killed all the Jews in Europe, except for a few people like them. I only know this because Joannie Olson told me this on our one date.

"You know Freddy's parents were in prison," she said during a slow dance while eyeing Brian Hodges, her real boyfriend, dancing with another girl.

"What do you mean in prison? What did they do?" I asked.

"They were Jews."

"That's a reason? I thought Jews made a lot of money?"

"The Germans put the Jews in prison and starved them to death. Justin, don't you know anything?" She said. Joannie had a way of saying stuff that made you feel really stupid. I am not sure why I had a crush on her but I did at the time.

"Why did they do that?" I asked.

"Because everyone hates the Jews." She said matter of factly.

"Well, I don't. I don't even know many Jews."

"Oh, half of Westport is Jewish."

"Get out of here, Joannie," I said and I meant it.

"My father told me and he doesn't make stuff up like you."

"What do I make up?"

"You never tell the truth, Justin."

She sort of had me there because I rarely did tell the truth especially around girls. I might have been the biggest liar at Bedford Elementary School. Most of the stuff I have already told you is the truth but how are you gonna know anyhow? Look it up in the encyclopedia?

I decided to meet Freddy at Thompson's Pharmacy. My mother wouldn't let me take my bike downtown because there too many cars and most people from Westport drove like maniacs anyhow. So I had to walk down Cross Highway and I stopped by the ole Merritt Superette to get some Chicklets. I loved the green and yellow Chicklets but I wasn't really crazy about the black or red ones. I am not real sure why. It was about another mile to Thompson's where I was suppose to meet Freddy to have some French fries and a cherry coke. We did this all the time after school but in the summer it was sort of unusual. It was like a date with a guy. Really sort of uncool stuff.

Fred was waiting and already sucking down his cherry coke. Fred was about my size which meant he was a pip squeak. He was better looking than me but dressed sort of crummy and was poor and all so the girls backed off him. Welcome to elementary school in Westport. Junior high would probably be worse.

"Hey, Freddy." I said.

"Hey, Justin. You took your sweet time getting here." Freddy did a lot of griping for a twelve year old kid. I guess since he was the kid of parents that survived prison and all I figured maybe he had a bad view of life. I was sort of a complainer too so we got along okay.

"I stopped for some candy."

"You get me any?"

"Why would I do that?"

"You got all the money, Justin. Your parents are rich."

"Yeah, right. That's why I am a lawn service instead of laying around the beach all day."

Freddy couldn't say much back about that although maybe he was embarrassed his mother ironed my shirts. It was a funny town we lived in. There seemed to be a lot of judging of others going on. Most people had a lot to say about other people if you know what I mean

"You wanna come over?" Freddy asked.

There really wasn't much to do at his house and it meant going past *The Twilight Zone* building.

"No, thanks."

"Are you still scared of the Fine Artist School?"

"I am not really afraid. It spooks me out though."

"You are sort of a chicken, you know that, Justin?"

I certainly knew that. I didn't wear a batting helmet designed by a jet pilot for nothing but I didn't like it coming from Freddy.

"And you are such a brave kid? You whimpered when you had to give an oral report in Mrs. Weigel's class."

"Did not."

"Did so. I was there."

"I am not a coward."

"You just say that because your parents survived prison and all."

"Who told you that?"

"Joannie Olson."

This shut Freddy up for awhile. While Joannie was a complete brat, she was cute and this carried a lot of weight among the boys.

"What was with that anyhow?"

"With what?"

"Your parents being in prison?" I asked.

"In concentration camps, Justin. You got a problem with that?"

"I got no problem with it. All I asked was why?"

"Cuz they are Jews, dummy."

"That seems pretty dumb."

"Most people hate Jews."

"Who?"

"The Germans for one."

I wasn't a very good debater. I had to admit this. I doubted all Germans hated Jews. My father once said he had a big nose and wasn't Jewish. He thought it was some kind of joke but when looks are important to a kid, you don't joke about the size of your nose. Freddy didn't have a big nose anyhow.

"Our neighbor is German. The Kruegers. They don't hate Jews."

"How do you know?"

"I don't really." I was being honest. Actually the Kruegers hated everyone.

"There are a lot of Jews in Westport and that is why we came here to live."

"Really?" I asked.

"That was what my father told me," Freddy said and he got sort of misty for a moment like he was going to cry.

"You might be the only Jew I know," I said.

"Thanks, Justin. But I doubt that."

"Well, I guess there is Murray Rosen."

"How is Murray doing?" Freddy asked.

"He is in the loony bin at Hallbrook."

"Figures." Freddy said.

Chapter 16

Teddy Newhouse had been my friend since 2nd grade. He lived in an apple orchard north of Cross Highway. His parents owned land that went clear through to the Nike fence. If I haven't mentioned it before Westport had its own army base full of nukes right next to the high school. It was sort of cool going through the rows of apple trees and right up to the Nike fence. Then they would yell at us to get the hell out of there. I guess they worried we would steal some top secrets and give them to the Russians or something. They weren't real nice to us but I guess they didn't like much living in tiny houses in rich Westport. Teddy was the opposite of just about everybody I knew. He was sort of fat for a kid, never studied and really didn't give a hoot about what anybody thought about him which was rare for Westport. Teddy used to wander all around the roads of town. He just walked everywhere. People didn't much notice him but he was always around. He went to Coleytown Elementary but I hadn't seen him all school year when he walked up Hitchcock Road to our house. I just got back from having lunch with Freddy. I was sort of sad about Freddy and his Jewish problem, so Teddy was kind of a relief.

Teddy stuck his big hand out to shake mine.

"How ya been, Justin?" He asked. He might as well have had on bib overalls and a stick of grass in his mouth the way he came across as a good ole boy farmer. But Teddy was exactly that. A farmer in Westport. Sort of funny when you thought about it.

"I've been good, Teddy," I said. I found I got talking like Teddy when I was around him. My mother thought Teddy was "odd" and I guess he was compared to everybody else.

"You like Bedford?" He asked. Teddy wasn't much for school and was often absent in the fall months when we were at Coleytown. Somebody said he was probably bringing in the harvest but I never asked.

"Junior High now. You going to Long Lots?" I asked. Teddy sat down on our island of manicured grass. The island was in the middle of a big gravel circle of a driveway. I gotta tell you I hated that gravel. Every winter we had to shovel the snow off it and every spring we had to pick the tiny gravel stones out of the grass and put them back in the driveway. Everybody else had tarred driveways.

"I may quit," he said.

"Will they let you do that?" I asked.

"If'n my parents say it's okay, I think."

"Your parents are gonna let you quit school after the 6th grade?"

"Why not? Ain't learnin' nothing."

Teddy had me there. I wasn't learning much either. Maybe a lot about goofing off in class and how to avoid doing my homework but not much else unless you include going steady with Betsy

Firestone. I still didn't know what that was all about either.

"What are you going to do all the time?" I asked. I was beginning to get interested in this new maverick Teddy Newhouse.

"I want to own my own farm. Somewhere far away. Where it is always warm. Like Hawaii maybe."

I thought for a moment. I had never had such thoughts. Growing up in Westport, you were expected to do well in school, go on to college and then get a job, get married and have kids. No one told you this was the way it had to be done, but everybody knew it.

"What are you going to farm, Teddy?" I asked.

"Maybe coffee. I hear it grows real good out there."

"Where did you hear that from?"

"Oh, I don't know, Justin. I hear all sorts of stuff you preppie kids never hear about."

And Teddy was right. He did hear a lot of stuff

that nobody ever talked about in our house or in school even.

"I ain't no preppie, Teddy. You know that. But I never did hear much about what you are talking about."

"I'm farm people. You are city people."

"I was born in Connecticut."

"I was born in the house I live in."

"I don't think my mother would have gone for that!" I joked.

"This town is going to the dogs is what my father said."

"They just named it an All-American city."

"Who did?"

"I think my father said Look Magazine."

"Never heard of it. Westport ain't no city anyhow."

"You don't read much, Teddy. No offense."

"I work."

"So do I. I got a lawn service. Five lawns I do every week."

"Well, you ain't like the other ones, Justin. That's why I hang out with you."

"Don't do me no favors, Teddy."

"What now? I got your hair up over this stupid town?"

"I like it here. Maybe if you played Little League or went to some of the dances, you might like it more too."

"Ain't got time for it."

"You got time to sit here talking about it."

"Got a point there. I should be moving on."

"You want to stay for dinner." I really didn't mean this for it took about an order from President Eisenhower to get anybody invited to our house for much of anything unless it was some guy from South America with my Dad's work.

"Naw, I got chores to do before supper."

"Ah, stay around for awhile, Teddy."

"What for?"

"I like to hear what you have to say."

"I got nothing to say."

"You do too. I like what you have to say."

"Nothing new."

"What do you think about Kennedy?"

"Who?'

"John Kennedy is running for President."

"I don't worry about that stuff."

"How come?" I asked.

"Cuz it does no good. They don't care much about what we folks care about anyhow."

"Why do you say that?"

"We got a Nike site in my backyard. Ain't it pretty clear?"

"I guess maybe you are right. So you don't like Nixon either?"

"I heard he's a crook."

Chapter 17

On August 1st, my father bought a new car. A 1960 Chevrolet Corvair. While the Ford Station Wagon was new to us it had been owned by a guy who had worked with my father and had moved to South America. So with the new Corvair, Beau, the 1952 Buick, had gone to the junk yard. Beau cried POOR when anybody saw it. It was black with rust all over it. In Westport many people had one nice car and also a "station car" they only drove to the train station. Beau was good for that, but my father liked to drive it all over especially if it snowed. So, if a party or dance was going on at the YMCA I could be sure to be picked up by ole Beau. Most of us guys would sit outside on the steps of the Y and check out cars. We always had some kind of knock on any car. Few were spared. And we were pretty nasty too. I usually told my parents to pick me up late so I would be the last one waiting for a ride.

The new Corvair was pretty cool though. It was small with bucket seats and a stick shift, like a racing car. My father had ordered one in gold, which was pretty odd for him. Going from black to gold was a big change for him. The Corvair was the first of its kind and my father thought he was pretty cool too. I didn't really care either way as long as Beau was gone. The Corvair didn't exactly say "money" but it was pretty cool looking.

"This will be your car to drive in high school," my father said. My first thought was that I might not make it to high school.

"If Duff doesn't wreck it first," I said.

"I was the youngest of 8 children, Justin, don't tell me about hand me downs. I will insure your brother takes good care of this baby."

Baby? What happened to good ole Dad? Did he have a girlfriend or something. Westport was the home of "Peyton Place" after all.

"I am sure you will, Dad. Thanks."

"You are welcome, Justin."

I could tell my father loved driving the sort of sports car. It had a four gear stick shift which my father didn't seem to know how to use because it made a grinding noise.

"What is that noise?" I asked as we passed the bridge downtown.

"Just the engine getting used to being driven." He replied. "Gotta break in the baby."

"Shall we take a drive down toward Longshore and the beach?" He asked. My father loved to drive around the town of Westport and witness the town properties and the big houses down by the beach. So did a whole bunch of other people.

"Damn New Yorkers," my father said as he beeped the horn at a big oversized Cadillac. I didn't know much about how a car worked, but I knew one car from another. Michael Babkie and I used to have a contest at the bus stop at Reichart Circle before school naming the various cars. I was pretty good at it too. Michael was better.

"This is a Chevrolet, right, Dad?" I asked him like he knew everything about cars.

"Yes, sir, this baby is right off the assembly floor at General Motors. It might be the first Corvair ever," he said with pride. He was even driving faster than usual.

"What is that stick thing for?"

"That is for sports cars, Justin. Gives it more power."

"How did you learn to drive it?"

"It is basically the same as the Buick, but the gear shift is on the floor instead of on the steering column. You have to use a clutch."

"The Ford is an automatic."

"Yeah, and it is a worthless automobile. You know what Ford stands for?" He asked.

"Ford Motor Company?" I answered.

"Figure On Repairs Daily," and he gave out a big laugh. He was really in a jovial mood.

"Why did you buy the station wagon then?"

"Your mother liked it," he groaned.

"I like this car much better."

"So do I!" He said and he gunned the engine down the road into Longshore Golf Course.

There was a guard house at the fork as you entered Longshore Park. It was meant to keep New Yorkers out, but nobody would say that. Longshore had once been a private country club, home to the real rich people like Elizabeth Taylor and Babe Ruth. Now the town owned it. But it was no normal country club. It not only had a golf course, but also a huge hotel, tennis courts, a marina and a big swimming pool full of salt water. Westport was home to many New Yorkers. Most got out of the city in the summer, but many came out just for the weekend.

Since most of Westport's men worked in New York, I guess they didn't want to hang around with New Yorkers on the weekends. Or the summer. Because Westport didn't much like New Yorkers, my brother told me the cops used to tow away any car with New York plates down at the beach. Just to be mean.

"Can I help you, sir?" The guard asked from his little house at the fork in the road by the ole Colonel's house by the 5th green. The guy sat perched on a bar chair. He wore some sort of uniform and looked to be in high school or maybe a little older. His hair was in a greasy crew cut, large black framed glasses and some nasty pimples on his face.

"We are just going to take a ride around the course, son," my father said really nice in his fake Westport voice.

"You need a car sticker for that," the kid answered. He was sort of a lazy wise guy kind of kid. The worst.

My father realized his mistake. Beau, the Buick now an assortment of steel parts at the junkyard, had the beach and town pass on its windshield.

"I just bought this car . . . "

"It is very nice, sir, but you need a Westport sticker to get into Longshore."

"I am a Westport resident."

"You still need a sticker."

"I have lived in Westport for 8 years now," my father insisted.

"You still need a sticker." The kid was stubborn.

"Maybe if you call First Selectman Baldwin..." My father suggested.

"There is no phone in here. Don't matter much if there was, I wouldn't make the call."

"What is your name, son."

"I ain't your son. And you don't have a sticker. Move your car."

"Or what?" My father asked.

"I will call the cops."

"You don't have a phone."

My father gunned the engine, slipped the gear shift into first and took off. Fast. I smiled to myself. I could see myself doing this one day.

Chapter 18

The Marauders were still undefeated after nine games and I was batting .312. Not bad for an Alfred E. Newman look-a-like and an outright shrimp. I was feeling pretty good about myself. I really was.

We played the Giants for the American League championship. The Giants were 7-2, so the game was sort of nothing. But the hot shots in Westport like to give stuff real importance. They like to go to their offices in New York City and tell everyone that their kid was playing in the "championship" game this weekend. The American League came from all the new houses in the area near Coleytown School. There was a ton of houses being built up where we lived up off Cross Highway and near Easton Road. Westport was becoming a real popular spot, I guess. I am not sure what the farmers like Teddy's family thought about it, but my father told me a lot of people were getting sick of the city with all the criminals and bad schools. I had been to New York City a couple of times and it was pretty noisy and smelly. If it was low tide on the Sound, Westport stank too but it was quiet.

The Giants were a good team with a strong pitcher. Jeremy Mullins was their star and their number one pitcher. You were only as good as your pitcher in Little League. It is really true. I made it up but it is true. The Marauders had two really good pitchers and that is why no one could beat us. The Giants had Mullins. I knew Jeremy well or at I thought I did. We used to go over to Timmy Wayne's house after school to swim in his next door neighbor's pool. It was Paul Newman's, the actor guy. I never saw any of the films he was in but he was a pretty big hot shot type of guy. I never saw him but my mother loved picking me up then cuz she liked all those actor kind of guys. Jeremy was a nice guy but his father was a jackass. There were a lot of those kinds of fathers in Westport. Driving around in their convertible hot shot cars and usually drinking booze like crazy. I saw many of them getting off the train drunk when my mother would take me to pick up my father. My Dad never drank much. My mother told me he once came home from work all drunk and all and he said it would never happen again. And it didn't. He was that kind of guy. When he said he was going to do something, he stuck to it. It was a pretty good way to be I guess.

I hadn't seen Jeremy Mullins in nearly a year. Westport chose to "redistrict" a bunch of us Coleytown kids to Bedford Elementary. I may have told you this already but I am telling you again. I didn't make much of a fuss about it but looking back it sort of stank to high heaven. It also meant my friends from Coleytown would be going to Long Lots Junior, the big time rival of Bedford Junior High where I was headed in a month or so.

Mullins was warming up when I crossed the diamond after infield practice before the game. He had gotten bigger in the year. He was never very tall but was heavy and had big legs. You could tell he was going to be a big guy one day. I waved to him but he ignored me. Not a good sign but maybe he didn't recognize me. But I certainly hadn't grown. I think I looked pretty much the same. Guys who don't wave back at you kill me. They really do. They know who you are but they are trying to be cool or something by thinking they are some kind of hot shot.

My first time at bat, I hit the first pitch up the middle for a single. Hodges bunted me to second and Mike Stevenson hit a double off the right field fence. This hitting kept going on when Bob Montenaro hit a home run over the center field fence. It was 3-0 before Mullins could get three outs.

It started in the first inning while we were in the field. Mullins became a real jerk.

"Hey monkey. Yeh, you at short stop. Monkey ears."

It was loud and Mullins stood on the top step of his dugout. There seemed to be complete silence as he continued with his insults.

"Monkey ears. Look at the short stop. A monkey can't field."

I looked briefly at Hodges. He was crouched down but his eyes were focused on Mullins. Even our pitcher Mike Stephenson looked different and slowed up on his pitches.

"Where's your Mama, monkey ears? Is she a gorilla?" He yelled.

"That's enough talk, young man," the umpire said as he stood at the back stop and stared at Mullins.

Mullins obeyed but it was not too long before he started up again.

After I fielded a ball and threw the runner out at first, he was at it again.

"Hey, monkey ears, you stink. You know that.

You stink. You stink so bad, you're smelling up the whole ball park."

And then it happened. Mike Stephenson put the ball on the rubber block in the pitching mound and walked off the field. Montenaro followed, then Rossi from behind the plate, then Thompson from first base and finally Hodges from second. They walked slowly. Heads down. No one said anything. No one looked at Mullins. I finally followed. The outfield of DeVries, McCarthy and Corrigan were right behind me. I felt like crying but I wasn't gonna let Mullins see me.

Coach Hotchkinson stood at the end of the fence watching all of us file passed him. He was a slender man with an expressionless face. But for this moment, he had a slight grin.

"Play ball, Coach." The umpire demanded.

"We forfeit, ump," was all he said.

The umpire nodded his head up and down in agreement and walked off the field. Mullins didn't say anything. A few Giants started a slight hurray of victory but it not for long. The crowd was quiet.

Then Mr. Mullins came forward. He was a thin, tall man with a deep tan. Sort a Kookie Burns of 77 Sunset Strip sort of guy. The type of guy who drives a convertible and flirts with all the ladies. He did just that too. I know because I saw him around town doing it. I can be a goofball but I am pretty aware of a lot of things.

Mr. Mullins was moving fast and everybody starting watching him as he walked the narrow corridor between the first base fence and the bleachers. You could tell he was not happy. He stormed through the entrance gate and stood looking into the Giants' dugout. And he found him. Quickly. He went into the dugout, pushing through the other players, looking at Jeremy. He pushed their manager out of the way and grabbed Jeremy by the front of his uniform. I could see everything and I knew what was coming. A severe slap across the face.

"You are gonna to apologize to Justin right now!" Mr. Mullins screamed. I was surprised that he remembered my name. I had been to dinner a couple of times but Mr. Mullins was usually pretty drunk or gone.

He yanked Jeremy by the arm and began to drag him across the dirt of home plate. There was a huge crowd now. No one was going to miss out on this drama. Except me. I sneaked out the back gate of the home team dugout and was gone through the woods before either Mullins could get close.

Some of my teammates later told me that Jeremy was crying his eyes out and Mr. Mullins slapped him a couple of more times before he was able to say he was sorry to the whole team. They all turned their backs to the Mullins.

Kids could be just as cruel in Westport as their parents.

Chapter 19

Joey Levi lived down by the river right behind the Merritt Superette. Joey wasn't cool or anything but since he was a short runt like me we got to know each other. Funny how little guys stuck together. Also Joey's parents liked to throw parties to make him popular and all which in a way worked. Joey was short with a crew cut, a long face and a jelly belly. He was sort of like a munchkin, if you know what that is.

The party got me excited especially after the Mullins game. I needed a pick me up and I knew Betsy Firestone was going to be there. This set up my problem of not knowing what to do with Betsy now that we were going steady. I wasn't really sure how I was supposed to act around Betsy. I mean we were officially going steady so she was my girl. I don't mean like she was some sort of slave girl of mine. My mother would kill me. But was I supposed to be with her the whole party? Dance with only her? The Scully party had not taught me anything. Thanks to Quincy.

I got there early because I could ride my bike. It was the long nights of summer and Joey's was only 2 miles away. I would have liked to be dropped off by Dad in the new Corvair but he was taking my mother out to dinner probably to show off his new car at the Patterson Club. My mother was going to pick me and my bike up with the station wagon at ten o'clock which was a little early for a party but those were her rules.

I got there on time and Hodges, Hopkins, and Oliver were all there but there were very few girls.

"Where are the girls?" I asked Hodges.

"You mean Betsy?" He asked. Brian had not said anything about the Mullins incident and I assumed he was keeping his mouth shut about it. Most of Little League stuff stayed on the team which was fine by me.

"We are going steady," I announced proudly.

"She's coming. I think with Joannie," Steve added.

I took a look around. The house was right on the river and practically falling into it. They had Christmas lights strung about the few trees in the tiny back yard and food was on a picnic table. This was definitely not going to be a make-out party. They had a transistor radio set up with some music but it was very loud. It was pretty kiddie like for some of Westport's finer kid parties but Joey was sort of lame anyhow. I liked him though. I really did.

"What time does it get dark now anyhow?" I asked no one in particular.

It actually got dark about nine o'clock I learned. I didn't really feel cool about making my "move" on Betsy until it was dark. I am not sure but that is how I felt. There was something about the dark that made goofballs like me feel sort of relaxed. A dark den in a basement was okay.

"You wanna dance?" I asked Betsy, who stood alone by the small dock.

"There isn't any music, Justin."

"Oh. Okay."

"How come you have been avoiding me?" She asked as she turned to look at me. She was about my height so it was a straight on stare.

I looked away. "I don't know." I murmured.

"I heard about the game yesterday."

"We forfeited, but we are still in the championship game," I answered.

"No, I mean about the terrible kid."

"You mean Jeremy Mullins?" I asked feeling sorry for myself.

"I guess. He was mean to you. I am sorry." She looked liked she was going to cry.

And then I kissed her. Smack dap right on the lips right there by a dock on the banks of the Saugatuck River. It was my first real kiss with Betsy and my first kiss with my steady girl. I was in sort of heaven and didn't have a boner or anything but was feeling really sexy.

That is until Quincy Smollin pushed us both into the water.

He came from nowhere at a moment I was thinking about some tongue action as well. I had never "French" kissed during any of the long make-out parties. But with Betsy everything was different. We hit the water together after a blind side from Quincy. I should have seen it coming. Quincy was a creep and I should have done something bad to him after the Scully party. Now, I was really mad. But right now, there wasn't much I could do about it. The water was well above my head and I treaded water while attempting to hold Betsy up. She was a good swimmer but swimming in a dress or fully dressed makes it hard. Quincy had disappeared from the dock area anyhow and I was hoping Dale Hopkins was chasing his butt all the way home. I bet Dale would do that for me too.

"Are you two okay?" Mrs. Levi asked, standing with two towels and a frown on her face.

I helped Betsy on to the dock and Mrs. Levi quickly wrapped a towel around her. You could see right through Betsy's dress and I did notice she was wearing a bra and black panties. I nearly had an instant boner but the cold water held it back. I lifted her out and wondered why girls clothes are see- through when wet while guys are not. Mrs. Levi took Betsy inside while talking about some dry clothes. I was left standing in my wet clothes in water up to my knees.

Steve Oliver sat at the end of the dock. Looking at the water.

"Damn that Quincy, why does he hate me so much?" I asked.

Steve didn't respond.

"What's wrong with you?" I asked.

"Anne Daniels just broke up with me."

It surprised me. I felt a chill. I climbed from the water and sat down on the dock. My shoes were ruined. I would hear about this from my mother. They were pretty new.

"Why did she do that?" I asked again.

Steve looked up. His eyes were filled with tears. "She said I was too short." And for some strange reason I couldn't help but laugh.

Chapter 20

I did catch hell for ruining my brand new loafers in the river, but I didn't get it right away. That usually meant I was off the hook. One time I got suspended for breaking a girl's pen at Coleytown. The principal booted me for a half a day but to my father it was like I killed someone. I had to rake the leaves at the school for three weekends in a row. If you messed up in our family you got it quick or not at all. I guess because my father had a lot of stuff on his mind and my mother never really liked to punish us kids.

We were off to our annual summer visit to my Aunt Ada's. We went once a year to Massachusetts, close to Sturbridge Village, a tourist spot equal to no other in boring any kid to death. Ada was my father's youngest sister and also the youngest of 8 children. My father spoke to maybe 2. I had met only this 1 sister. His 6 brothers were strangers. It was sort of weird but nobody ever dared ask my father why. He was kinda private that way. Maybe he was sort of embarrassed about his poor childhood. I guess maybe his brothers reminded him of how crappy he had it as a kid. He worked pretty hard to live in a fancy place like Westport so I guess he could do what he wanted. I sure didn't plan on hanging around with my brother when I got older. Of course the way I was headed I would probably end up poor and living on the streets somewhere.

Ada was fat and sort of ugly. I know that is mean to say about your own Aunt but she really was. She sort of looked like a woman version of my father. Uncle Arthur, Ada's husband, was another story. He was a wild man and how he ended up with Ada is beyond me. The only good thing about visiting Ada's house was being around Uncle Arthur. He was a big man, tall and well built. He might have passed for a weight lifter at one time but his gut was now big. He wore big black glasses and had a very tiny mustache which curled at the very ends. Uncle Arthur would always greet my brother and me by shaking hands. He would transfer 5 dollars this way without my parents knowing. He did this upon our arrival and departure. So 10 bucks was worth a weekend in Massachusetts anytime anyhow. No matter how boring.

The sort of cool thing about visiting the Champlins (that was their name) was the arguing between my mother and Aunt Ada. I never really thought of my mother as a snob. Actually she was sort of an anti-snob snob in Westport but in the Champlin household she had her nose stuck clear through the ceiling. She and Aunt Ada would go at it on just about everything.

"Looks like you may have gained some weight," Aunt Ada said out of the blue to my mother. Ada really looked up to her brother, my father, and didn't think any woman was good enough for him. My mother was trying to prove her wrong at every turn.

"Exact same weight I was when I got married," my mother responded.

"More to love," my father joked as he chocked down some big bad hamburgers Arthur was grilling out on the porch. Arthur loved to grill. And he did. Just about everything.

"You look like you have lost a pound or two," my mother answered Aunt Ada.

"Oh, no! Arthur likes his women big."

"Well, he should be happy with you," my mother said. Aunt Ada looked the other way.

My brother and I were usually sent off to the television room or the back yard to play football or baseball but we did like to listen in on the conversations. A lot of it was about when my father and Aunt Ada were kids growing up on a farm. It sounded pretty cool compared with Westport but you could tell my mother didn't approve. I think she felt herself above all that poverty stuff since her parents got a new car every year and vacationed in Florida during the winter. The Carmichaels were dirt farmers from Rhode Island with too many mouths to feed and a damn lousy place to farm anything. My Grandpa eventually had to go to work at a mill to support everybody. It was sort of a sob story and all, but it couldn't have been easy growing up like that. I guess that was why father was sort of a task master and cheap.

"Does anybody want more cake?" Aunt Ada asked.

"No, I couldn't eat another bite," my mother said. She probably meant because the cake was crummy which it was. Never mess with my mother when it comes to baking.

"I will have some more," Uncle Arthur said. Considering Uncle Arthur probably weighed close to 300 pounds his response wasn't a surprise.

"You will have to give me the recipe," my mother snarled at Aunt Ada.

"It's store bought," she responded.

"Oh," my mother said aghast. "With all the time you have, I thought it would be home made."

Another dagger to Ada's heart. Women could be fierce! Worse than the worst 12 year old Westport kid around but I was up there in the rankings.

"I am quite busy, Norma, I will have you know."

"Try having two kids and a job."

"Must be difficult in Westport."

"No more than any other place even Sturbridge," my mother answered. This is when my lame brother and I usually got sent outside, but not this time.

"Oh, you Westport snobs, you think we all have nothing to do in the sticks of Massachusetts."

"Hardly snobs we are just better than most people," my mother answered. Another zinger to the soul. My mother despite her obvious snobbery was dishing it out today. My brother and I giggled in the television den.

"That's enough, ladies," my father said.

"What are you talking about, Randolph?" My mother asked sternly.

"I am tired of hearing you two fight."

"Then leave!" my mother commanded.

There was a silence in the living. Uncle Arthur was not getting his third piece of cake.

"Don't you tell my brother to leave my house!" Aunt Ada countered. Her Irish temper was lathered up good.

"Don't you tell me anything!" My mother responded. "Boys, we are leaving! Boys! We are leaving! Get your stuff! Now!!"

Uncle Arthur didn't say goodbye. No one came out to the car but my father with his head down tail between his legs.

I didn't get my goodbye 5 bucks either.

Chapter 21

I had to get the missing Uncle Arthur 5 bucks because I wanted to get Betsy a gift. I figured I might go to Freddy English's father and buy her a necklace or something. It would be my way of helping out the Jewish people in town. Freddy let me know I was pretty lucky to have all the stuff I did and now a brand new Corvair and all. We weren't exactly rich but still you got to give something back.

I had my steady lawn service with three lawns off Cross Highway and ours. Each took a half of day to do. Ours took me an entire day. I got 3 bucks a lawn per week while my father paid me $2.75. I got no idea why we agreed on that price but I think my father was pretty cheap compared to a lot of others in town. He also had me write up a contract which was my first real try at writing. He sent it back once because there was nothing about if he didn't like the job I had done. No kidding. My father could be a pretty big jerk when it came to not liking stuff.

Today's job was at the tip of Cross Highway by the big hill leading to Main Street. It was right down the street from where the guy had hung himself a couple of years ago. I delivered the Bridgeport Post to that guy's door every afternoon. One day I rode my bike across his lawn and saw him hanging in his green house. It was like a bad movie or a nightmare. My mother called the police and all but I didn't stay around long. It was sort of sad and nasty. It really was. If you have ever seen anybody dead before you would know what I mean. It gives me the creeps even talking about it. Worse than *The Twilight Zone*.

I had to get a ride down to this customer's house because it was about a half mile from our house. My mother took the station wagon and all and didn't seem too upset about the weekend fight with Aunt Ada. I think she sort of liked to get into it with ole Aunt Ada instead of mostly talking about the weather with us. My father had this thing about rotator blade lawn mowers so we owned this old reel cutter machine. It worked okay but weighed like a thousand pounds. My mother had to help me get it in and out of the station wagon. She wasn't too happy about that but she did help. She was really huffing and puffing as she helped me. Those Pall Malls were killers. I didn't say anything though.

We got down to this house and the lawn is like 2 feet tall.

"When was the last time you mowed this lawn?" My mother asked, grunting as she helped get the mower out of the back of the car.

"Last week," I said.

"Last Monday?"

"I don't think so, Justin. You had a game that night. You haven't worked all week."

"Then it was two weeks ago." I said.

"Maybe, like three weeks ago. It's a regular wheat field out there."

After my mother left and I tried three times to start the antique mower Mr. Harding came out. He was the owner of the property and a tall, skinny kind of guy with bib overalls and a corncob pipe. He didn't look like the guy they would choose to be on the Westport All-American city poster that's for sure. He was a pretty good guy though.

"You got to choke that machine, son." He said, puffing on the pipe and walking my way. I had a thing about people calling me "son." If a teacher did, it usually meant he was a jerk.

"I have it choked, Mr. Harding."

"Then you flooded it."

"Whatever you say."

"Son, where you been? This grass ain't been mowed in nearly a month."

"I was here two weeks ago."

"We agreed on once a week." He said. Another guy like my father.

"I have been busy."

"Doing what may I ask?"

"My grandfather died."

"That was in early July."

This caught me slightly off guard. I hardly knew the Hardings and I know my parents didn't. I suspected he had called the house. I was a pretty good liar under pressure but he was one up on me.

"That was my mother's father. My Dad's father passed away just last week." See?

"I am sorry to hear that," Mr. Harding said. I knew he didn't believe me and I also knew that adults don't screw around with death. I thought I was back on top.

"But that reel mower ain't gonna cut all that tall grass out there. You are gonna need a sickle."

"I don't have a sickle," I said. Nor did I know what one was.

"I got one in the back. You play golf?"

"Yes, sir."

"Good, you can practice."

And so, an entire day was spent swinging the sharp sickle against the tall grass. All because my mother couldn't get along with Aunt Ada and I didn't get 5 bucks from Uncle Arthur. It did mean I could get Betsy a nice gift though. I think I was sort of falling in love her cuz I thought about her a lot. And I don't mean in the jerking off kind of way. I just thought things about her. It was sorta nice.

Chapter 22

The following day, August 7th to be exact, everything went crazy in our household. My mother woke me up and my brother was crying.

"What's going on?" I asked crawling out of bed still sore from working hard with the sickle. It took me five hours to do the Hardings' lawn.

"Castro has taken over the U.S. Rubber factories in Cuba!" My brother bellowed. "Dad might lose his job!"

This was the kind of guy my brother was. He could have been Eddie Haskell on *Leave It to Beaver*. He was like that fake actor type. All wired up all the time. It was really getting on my nerves and I was glad he was getting his own room.

"Did Dad tell you that?"

"I saw it on television. Castro is taking over everything because of the embargo."

"Oh," I said, not having any idea of what an embargo was.

"Mom said Dad is drinking up a storm."

"It's 10 in the morning!"

"I guess they are going crazy at the office." The office was in New York City on the Avenue of the Americas. I had been there once and saw his big hot shot office with his secretary named "Margaret" who got everything for him. Sort of like what Mom did for him at home. She wasn't real good looking though. She has this big mole on her chin. It was almost the size of a ping pong ball. It was really sort of disgusting. Not in the way like a dead guy hanging himself but the kind where you wouldn't have lunch with her or anything. I mean sitting there staring at that mole while eating could make you throw up. I am sure she was a nice lady and all but she wouldn't have been my secretary for very long.

"Dad is a smart guy. I am sure he will find another job."

"Cuba and South America are his job."

"Well, I guess that means he has South America left." I knew Cuba was its own island because my father bought me a globe once and always showed me where he had been. It was pretty cool actually. The globe had a little light inside and I used to watch it in the dark and picture where he was at night when he was gone. I could get pretty sentimental that way sometimes. I really could.

"Cuba was his baby."

"Don't throw out the baby with the bath water," I replied, having no idea whatsoever that meant. My grandfather used to say it all the time and I found myself standing toe to toe with my brother in a conversation. Either he was getting a lot dumber or maybe I wasn't such a goofball after all.

"If Dad loses his job we are going to have to move."

"Why would that be?" I asked. I had no idea what he was talking about.

"Listen stupid . . ."

"Don't call me stupid. Mom told you not to."

"Listen, stupid, it costs a lot of money to live in Westport. Now, Dad makes a lot. If he loses his job we are out of here."

"Baloney."

"Baloney you, stupid."

And then I hit him. Right in the stomach.

"You asked for it," Duff said. And soon I was on the floor with my brother pounding me left and right. He pinned my arms down with his knees and was really whaling away at me. It wasn't the first time he had done this. Despite our love of sports and playing sports together, we really didn't have much else in common. Matter of fact, looking back on it all from my little room here at Hallbrook I don't think we liked each other very much.

After a few more blows to my cheeks my mother ran into the bedroom.

"Duff, get off your brother right now. Now!" And he did. "You two ought to be ashamed of yourselves. All this happening with your father's work and all and you are fighting."

"He started it," my brother said.

"I doubt that, Duff," my mother said and shut him up good.

"Is this going to change the election?" I asked. I figured it might be a good time to think about other stuff. Good stuff.

"Nixon will win."

"That's not what Mrs. McCarthy says."

"She is Irish, what do you expect?" My mother spat back and left the room.

My face was still hurting bad and my brother went over toward his own side of the room. He was taking his sweet time moving into the other bedroom. Making "it his own" as he put it. But that day, he stayed put. He picked up the National League All-Star baseball I had bought for him. He flipped it from one hand to the other.

"Wanna play some whiffle ball?" He asked.

My brother and me had not always been at each

other throats. He was actually Randolph, Jr. But I guess my grandfather didn't like his first grandson being called that so he gave him a nickname. "Duffer" was what they called lousy golfers. It stuck. Duff was two years older than me but a lot bigger. We played together all the time when he was younger and not such a jerk. We played football in the fall in the back yard. Tackle too and he killed me all the time. I was the Giants and he was the Colts. In the winter we used to sneak into the basketball courts at Bedford Elementary and play all day. I was the Knicks and he was the Celtics. In the summer we played whiffle ball in the back yard when my father was traveling or at Coleytown if he was home. He was the Red Sox and I was the Yankees. We never agreed on a team we liked. Never. I guess that should tell you something. Duff got good grades and I had problems in school. He was really good looking and I was Alfred E. Newman.

When he got to junior high he really became a

jerk. He started to act like a creep hanging around the Pilgrim Fellowship and all and wearing goofy kinds of clothes. You could tell a lot about a guy by the way he dressed in Westport then. They called it "preppie", but cool guys usually wore penny loafers and khaki pants with a dress shirt. The greasers wore boots and jeans with a shirt with no collars or sleeves. Duff was sort of in the middle with the way he dressed. He could play basketball pretty good so he was okay wearing what he wanted which was not real cool. But I knew down deep he could be pretty mean to me. Like today. He was a bastard.

So I just walked away from him.

Chapter 23

Freddy English called and wanted to go canoeing. That was a first. He said his mother would pick me up and we could go to Camp Mahackenoe and use some canoes. His sister was a camp counselor there and we could canoe down ole Saugatuck River to downtown. My very first thought was that we would have to go past the Famous Artist School and *the Twilight Zone*, but I didn't tell Freddy. It is one thing to be scared and another to be a baby and Freddy could have a pretty big mouth about stuff he thought was chicken. I guess this came from being brave and all after your parents have survived a concentration camp.

Freddy's mother was a short squat woman who apparently was making up for being in that camp by eating everything in sight now. She munched on a donut as she drove way too slowly in a beat up Ford Falcon. Freddy was very quiet during the ride and I could barely make out what his mother was talking about. I do think it was English, but it was sort of like the Ruskies talk if you know what I mean. My father brought big wigs from other countries home with him for dinner mostly from South America but a couple were from Africa. I could never understand a word they said even though they were talking in English. I became pretty good at blocking out everything I did not understand. I was very good at it. I did so in class all the time.

We got to the camp and I thanked Mrs. English like a maniac. I really did. I could be pretty polite if I wanted to be. At the camp we met Freddy's sister. I have forgotten her name but she was real good looking. Tall with red hair she was the opposite of Freddy. I sort of wondered if she was born before her parents went into the prison camp. Maybe Freddy was short like me cuz his mother didn't have enough to eat.

"You guys do know how to canoe, right?" Freddy's sister asked. I am pretty sure she was wearing a bra and her chest went up and down when she walked. I was feeling kinda of sexy just looking at her walk.

We both shook our heads. Freddy actually seemed to be afraid of his own sister. Maybe she had punched him around like my brother did me.

"Okay, then. Someone will pick you up down by the railroad station just after the bridge." I guess she didn't see us shaking our heads "NO" about using the canoe. Older kids are sometimes like that. They don't like to waste their time teaching you much of anything. My brother was like that. I would ask him a question and he would just call me "stupid." I would never find out the answer.

"How far is that?" I asked about where we were gonna get picked up. I had no idea how to canoe, but figured it can't be too difficult if Indians did it on television all the time.

"Oh, it just two miles or so. Easy sneezy." She

said. I could tell from the way she said it, it wasn't gonna be easy at all. Big shots always think it is going to be real easy cuz it is easy for them. It is a way of showing off. It really is.

I looked at Freddy and he seemed to be okay with it. I knew that it was two miles from the YMCA to my house and that seemed a long way. But I figured it had to be easier on the water than walking in the cold at night when your mother wouldn't pick you up.

"Just watch the rapids at the end of the lake just down there," she pointed, but I didn't see much. Rapids?

Freddy English got worse grades than I did so he was in the stupid category. Not that there is anything wrong with that but it can cause problems when you are canoeing down a river with rapids. Just as I thought. When we cast off from the Camp Mahackeno dock we were instantly lost. We went around in circles for about ten minutes and then finally just started floating with the current. Freddy sat in back. I sat in front paddling like a mad man.

"Nothing to this, hey, Freddy?" I yelled back. I was afraid to look back though. The fear of tipping the canoe over hit me the minute I got in it.

"I got it covered," Freddy responded.

"Have you ever canoed before?" I asked.

"Nope, you?"

I didn't answer. Any dummy could see I was lost.

"How deep is the water?" I asked.

"Over your head."

"How do you know?"

"You can tell by the color of the water. It is really deep here."

The one problem with Freddy other than being stupid was that he didn't know he was stupid. The color of the water was the same all the way down the Saugatuck River and even I knew the water could not be the same depth all the way down.

About half way down the river we saw another canoe. This was one of those wooden jobs that looked expensive. Freddy and me were doing pretty good with our canoe by now. Of course the current was doing most of the work but we were moving right along. As we got closer to the wooden canoe I could see two boys sitting there sort of waiting for us. And one was Quincy Smollin, the total jerk and slime ball.

"Freddy, turn us toward the left here."

"I think they call that the port. Or maybe it's the starboard." He replied.

"Don't get smart on me now, Freddy. That's Quincy over there and I hate him. In front of everyone he said I peed in Scully's pool when the water turned red from the red dye his father put in the pool."

"What did he do that for?" Freddy asked.

"Because he's a jerk."

"Paddle us left, will you?"

Freddy had no idea how to steer the canoe so we drifted right into Quincy and his expensive canoe.

"What are you guys doing?" Quincy yelled over to us although we were about ten feet from his canoe.

"Same thing you are doing." I replied with disqust.

"How far you going?" Freddy asked. I nearly swatted him one for talking to Quincy.

"We are just fooling around. Maybe do some fishing." The other guy was a stranger to me. He was much older and sort of a big guy. He had a cigarette hanging out of his mouth. Now while Michael Babkie and me had smoked my mother's Pall Malls and some of his father's cigars, I really didn't approve of smoking for kids. Only greaser kids smoked anyhow. They said it stunted your growth and I was too small already.

"You wanna come down the river with us?" Freddy asked. Damn it!

"We could race," Quincy said. Big man now with his big guy in the back of the canoe.

"Let's go!" I shouted and we were off.

Sort of. We were quickly coming to the part where it stopped being a river and started being a waterfall. The falls were only about 5 feet down but still they looked dangerous. And I was in the front.

"Freddy, waterfalls!" I shouted. Quincy's canoe was already ahead of us and the last thing we needed was to go fast over the falls.

"I got it covered, Justin. Just keep paddling." Freddy yelled back. It was hard to hear now. The waterfalls were making quite a sound. Like thunder. But just as we got inside 10 feet of the falls, a big swan came from our left. It was up on its feet like it was walking on the water and it looked angry. It made a strange sound like a fire alarm.

"Look out, Freddy, the bird!"

The swan rammed into the front part of canoe to the left. Port or starboard, I didn't care much. It came very close to ramming my head.

"Duck, Justin!" Freddy screamed. And just as he did, we tumbled over the falls and down into the flowing river.

And flipped over.

It was a good thing Freddy and me could both

swim cuz it was really deep. I took a mouth full of water and was coughing like a madman. There was some long grass stuff just a little to our left and we went over to that. It was all muddy and when we tried to walk in it, we sunk in the mud.

That jerk Quincy just kept going with his big friend and you could hear him laughing like the real jerk he was. I looked over at Freddy and he was crying.

"Freddy, you okay?"

"I'm scared, Justin. How are we going to get out of this? We might get eaten by snakes in this grassy stuff."

There are a few things that really scare me. A fast ball coming at my head and snakes are two big ones. So I did what every young kid from Westport would do.

I started screaming at the top of my lungs.

"Help! Help!" I yelled.

Chapter 24

That Saturday after being taken again to Doc Beinfield to be checked for some kind of disease from the Saugatuck River and the marshy area where the firemen had to come save us, we had the town championship game.

Marauders versus the Hornets!

It was the first time for this kind of game and nearly the whole town turned out. We played it at Coleytown and not at Gault Park down by the Saugatuck River. Thank God for that! Between the Levi party dunking and overturning the canoe, I had had enough of that river.

Mike Stephenson was on the mound for us. I think he pitched every game for us. He was good. Tommy Allen was on the mound for the Hornets. He was a big guy with a strong arm and the Hornets had some real hitters. Dale Hopkins played for them and I saw Dale hit a baseball into the woods at Gault Park. Not an easy task and maybe 350 feet away. Dale was sort of like our Bob Montenaro. Big and strong and born to bat.

Mike struck out all three batters in the top of the first inning to get us off to a great start. Their first pitch to me hit me on the elbow. I just ducked in front of the ball instead of backing away from it. Despite being a chicken at heart, this was a big game and I had to grow a pair of steel balls (with or without my steel cup) after nearly drowning in the Saugatuck River two days earlier. I took my base proudly and clapped hard for Brian Hodges now at bat.

"Take it deep," I yelled at Brian. Considering Hodges wasn't much bigger than me, he glanced my way with a look. Meanwhile I caught the sign from third base coach Mr. Corrigan. Steal!

In Little League you can't steal until the ball leaves the pitcher's hand and I timed it just right. The second the ball left Tommy Allen's right hand,

I was off in a hurry. I slid in before the tag by Tim Romano at second base. Most of the Hornets were from the Saugatuck area or ole Westport as some called it. I knew many of them from Longshore and the YMCA where you got to meet nearly every young kid in town.

The count was 3-2 on Hodges and he hit a little roller to third base on a bad pitch. The 3rd baseman charged and Tommy Allen tried to get to it but Brian was safe and I was on third base. Nobody out with the "heart" of our lineup coming up! Mike Stephenson batting left-handed hit a high fly ball to right field. It was crazy to me how far Mike could hit the ball with such an easy swing. The ball sailed to the right fielder and he made a good catch against the fence. Nice play but it allowed me to tag and score. 1-0 Marauders with Bobby Montenaro up to bat. Bobby was a man at 12 years old. He was a grade ahead of most of us so he was either very smart or started school early. I was betting the latter. He wasn't the sharpest knife in the dishwasher as my mother used to say. Bobby had been on fire but Tommy Allen had the best of him and struck him out with three pitches. Up came Brian Rossi, a good hitter and our star catcher. Brian was younger than anybody and also had a gorgeous sister which made him real popular. A lot of guys liked to spend the night at his house. Allen threw two curves that missed the plate and Rossi held off two fastballs that looked good but were called balls. Man on first and second. One out. This brought up Tommy Thompson, another left hander and our first baseman. Tommy was also a grade ahead and went to private school like Mike Stephenson. This meant he was smart and rich. On the first pitch, Tommy lined a shot to Tim Romano at second and he doubled up Hodges who was half way to third. Double play. End of the first.

The Hornets could not touch Mike Stephenson's fast ball during the first two innings and we couldn't touch Tommy Allen's curve either. Going into the third inning we were still up 1-0 with my run scored. I led off the third. Allen was throwing all curve balls now. The ball would head right at you and then swerve to the right. Most times he could get it over. With me he hit me with the first pitch for the second time. I would have ducked out of the way but I was getting tough. I would sacrifice body for the team! Hodges was up next and Brian lined a rare fast ball down the third base line for a single. Two on with Mike up. Allen's curve didn't work so well with left-handed batters. He tried to sneak a curve by Mike but couldn't do it. Mike took him deep with a blast over the right field fence and into the playground by Mrs. Wolfson's class. 3-0 Marauders.

Allen was replaced by Dale Hopkins. Dale was a good guy and big too but all he could do was throw fast balls. The first batter, Bobby Montenaro, bombed the first pitch over the center field scoreboard. It was like a bullet out of a gun. Bobby barely moved from the batter's box. 4-0 Marauders. Hopkins got the rest of the lineup out, 1-2-3. Dale was settling down to some serious fast balls.

In the top of the 4th, the Hornets came back on us. Mike let go of a couple of sloppy fast balls in the middle of the plate and the Hornet hitters pounced on them. Allen hit a shot to left field and then Dale hit a towering drive to the grassy area out beyond the left field fence and suddenly it was 4-2 Marauders. Bob Montenaro replaced Mike and struck out the other side. Everybody on our team knew that Bob was only good cleaning up things off the mound. His arm would be dead by the next inning. Allen remained sharp with a nasty curve and struck the bottom of our order out in the bottom of the fourth.

In the top of the fifth Bob was hit hard by the mighty Hornets. Paul Kennedy lined a shot off the left field fence and then their third baseman hit a double to right field where our Ralph Slater bobbled the ball and allowed Kennedy to score and the batter to reach third. I gave Ralph the evil eye but it didn't change things. It was a tied score with Dale Hopkins up. Hoppy, as we called him, hit another tremendous home run to the pasture beyond left field. He smiled at me as he turned second. I didn't smile back. Coach Hotchkinson decided to bring in Tommy Thompson to pitch. Bobby Montenaro went back to third base. Tommy, a left hander who pitched sidearm, baffled the Hornets and they were down 1-2-3 including a strike out by Tommy Allen. But we were down now 5-4.

In the bottom of the fifth, Tommy Thompson got on with a walk as Allen seemed to be getting tired. Brian Rossi hit into a double play and then Bruce Corrigan doubled off the left field fence. Peter DeVries pinch hit for our centerfielder, Kevin Cunningham, who was a terrible hitter, and hit the first pitch for a single to right center field. Corrigan ran like all get out and scored with a good slide to home. The score was tied at the end of 5 innings.

In a surprise move, Coach Hotchinson put

Bobby Montenaro back in to pitch. Since he hadn't been out of the game it was legal. The Hornets manager, a fat guy who looked like a cop, made a weak protest but the umpire brushed him aside. Bobby's arm came to life again and he struck out the first two batters. Dale Hopkins came to bat and with a 2-2 took a fast ball deep to left field. Bruce Corrigan went back to the fence, stood there and then grabbed it for the final out. Bottom of the sixth and final inning, tie score.

Ralph Slater was first up for us and he struck out on three pitches. Ralph was having a bad day but nobody felt sorry for him. Tommy Thompson was up next and lined one to left field. First pitch. Dale was showing signs of getting tired on the mound. Tommy McCarthy, the last in the order, came to bat. He fouled off two good fast balls. He took a good look at Coach Corrigan. Coach was whipping signs left and right across his chest, then to his cap and then to his nose. Bunt?

Sure enough, Tommy McCarthy laid down a

perfect bunt toward third base. Tommy Allen, now at third, charged hard and made a side armed throw. Tommy McCarthy was out, but Tommy Thompson was at second with two outs. The only problem was that I, the leadoff hitter, was up. I was shaking like a worm in the wind. I could barely keep my hands still on the bat.

Dale threw me a fast ball right down the middle of the plate. I was looking to walk if I could. I figured Brian could maybe get a hit better than me. The second pitch was way outside. I took a deep breath and wondered whether Dale was as nervous as me. He never looked nervous but I knew he had some deep feelings cuz he once told me about him and Ann Morehouse while we were in math class. It wasn't the talk of a big guy. It was more talking like he was a little shrimp like me. And so I figured if Dale could be nervous I could be too but I would try to hit him.

The next pitch was a fast ball right down the middle. I made a pass at it, but it was in the catcher's mitt before I could get around on it. Since Dale only threw fast balls I only now had to time it. The next pitch was the same and I went for it. Smack! A solid shot over the shortstop's head and into left field. A hit never felt so good. I was so shocked that I forgot to run.

"Go, Justin, go!" Someone yelled.

And I did. Tommy Thompson scored from second easily and the Marauders were the Little League champions of Westport!!!

Everybody ran out to meet me and grab me and put me on their shoulders. The whole crowd was going crazy. Not the Hornet fans, but everybody else. It was great!

One of the best days of my life.

Chapter 25

The best day of my life turned into the worst very quickly. We were having our Sunday dinner at exactly 2:00 PM following church services when the phone rang.

"Who is that?" My father asked annoyed.

"Obviously someone calling," my mother said dryly. Nearly as dry as her pot roast.

"Why would someone be calling at this hour?" My father asked.

"Would someone get that? Randolph, people do call during the day. You know that, correct?"

My father did not respond nor look up. He was busy trying to cut up the pot roast. He was a pretty hungry guy a lot of the time. No match for Uncle Arthur, but he could pack it away with the best of them. He may have sort of resented my mother's cooking.

"I will get it," my brother said and was off in a flash. I guessed he had a new girl friend not that many called our house but he had requested a phone in his room for "privacy" he said.

I could hear him in the kitchen. "Carmichael residence. Duff speaking. How may I help you?"

There was silence as we all listened carefully to his footsteps.

"It is for stupid." He said.

"Duff, I have told you many times not to call your brother stupid," my mother lectured.

"Especially after his day yesterday," my father said.

"Getting a hit doesn't take much brains," my brother answered.

I smacked him one on the biceps as I went for the phone. I took the phone on its long extension cord into the hall closet and closed the door.

"Lamumba." I said referring to Steve Oliver's and my nicknames for each other in reference to the African turmoil and its leader.

"I can't tell you my name," the girl's voice said.

I hesitated. A girl calling me? And I knew it wasn't Betsy. She had a kinda of deep voice like Pat Taylor who stabbed me. But I knew it wasn't Pat. She sorta hated me.

"I just called to tell you are not going to be popular anymore," the voice said.

I said nothing. She hung up.

I went back to the dinner table.

"Who was it, Justin?" My father asked. It looked like he had a piece of the roast beef stuck in his throat as he acted funny and making some grunting noises.

"It was a girl," my brother announced.

"Girls calling here? Oh, Justin, you must be the most popular boy in your class," my mother said proudly.

"I don't think so, Mom."

She smiled. My father spit out a piece of something.

The proof of the pudding, as my mother would say, came the next day. The Babkies had invited me to go out on their boat. Of course it was Michael's idea. Mr. and Mrs. Babkie didn't like me much since my fight with Peter that summer. They were okay but not really nice. Sort of a phony nice if you get my drift. Michael and I sat in the back seat of their station wagon. A Dodge. Big back seat. Mr. Babkie drove too fast and heard about it often from his very proper English wife.

"Slow down, Joe." She said.

"Stop the nagging, hey?" He replied. The big man had huge hands. None of his kids, Michael, Peter or Robbie, looked anything like him.

As we rounded North Compo at Darbrook Lane and headed down the slight hill, there stood Brian Hodges hitchhiking.

"Dad, that's our school friend. Stop!" Michael said. And he did.

Brian jumped in the back seat with Michael in between him and me. Brian didn't say anything to me and I knew that word was out. I had been put on some kind of shit list. The girl's call last night was merely a warning. Now the cold shoulder treatment would begin. I am not sure this was regular behavior or not. We usually just told somebody to their face that they were creepy and we didn't want to hang out with them anymore. This silent treatment was new. It was also worse.

We all three sat in the back seat for the ten minute drive to the beach area where Brian got out. He didn't say anything. He didn't even say "thank you" to the Babkies for the lift. He seemed really mad at something and I guessed it was me. Now if I wasn't a real chicken at heart I would have asked him. What's up? And who was that girl calling me yesterday. But like going steady with Betsy, I didn't really know what to say or do. I do know that I am writing all this down but I sure didn't know what to do or say on the phone or with Brian Hodges in the back seat of the Babkies car. I surely didn't.

"How come Brian wouldn't talk to you?" Michael asked in his always curious way.

I shook my head.

"Have you been exiled like Napolean?" Mrs. Babkie asked in her perfect English accent.

I shook my head. I felt like crying.

The boat ride did not help. The Babkies owned a large cabin cruiser, a motor boat. Joe Babkie liked to run the boat half way to Long Island. On today's cruise, the water was rough and I got sick almost immediately. There may be nothing worse than sea sickness. I was puking up the hot dogs I had after our win over the Hornets two days before. It was ghastly, I gotta tell you.

"Try some of this ginger," Mrs. Babkie offered. She was being nice for the first time since they moved next door nearly five years ago.

"Won't I puke that up too?" I asked.

"It will settle your stomach. Take some."

It didn't help much and I did throw it back up over the side of the boat. I didn't let anybody see so Mrs. Babkie did not have to feel bad about being wrong and all. I mean she was being nice. There was a cabin below and I lay down for the remainder of the trip. They drove me to the door when we returned to Hitchcock Road and made sure I got in okay. I was feeling a little bit better but was very light headed, almost dizzy.

"What is the matter with you?" My brother asked.

"Sick to my stomach," I moaned.

"You are such a faker."

"Why would I fake it?"

"You are always wanting sympathy," he said and he was gone.

I climbed the stairs to the kitchen and turned on the light. The kitchen was always dark and even in mid-summer daylight it was difficult to see. The house seemed empty. My parents would be playing golf since it was Monday afternoon because the whole town of Westport seemed to be on vacation.

I noticed an envelope on the kitchen table. It

merely said "JUSTIN" on the front. My heart started beating like crazy and I thought I was going to pass out. I really did. It was a worse feeling than when I jerked off and I didn't expect sudden relief this time. I sat down in the captain's chair. My father's seat at the table. I slid slightly on the padding of the chair. I always hated these chairs.

I picked up the envelope and felt it tear in the front. I opened it quickly and saw it was my Delta fraternity ring. Betsy had broken up with me.

I had to puke again.

Chapter 26

I have been in the Hallbrook nut house now for nearly two months. I lost so much weight before Labor Day my parents refused to send me to school. The phone calls had continued. Everyone seemed to want to tell me I was a creep now. My parents unplugged the old phone. Even Michael stopped coming around although I think he thought being a creep might be contagious.

I got to feeling so bad I tried to take a whole bottle of aspirin my parents kept in the hall closest next to the Brill Cream. I was feeling so down and out that I figured heaven must be better than Westport and all its phonies. One day they like you and are patting you all on the back and then the next, they hate you. I figured if Jesus loves you like Mr. Oliver kept telling us in confirmation class then he would take better care of me. I really didn't think I was gonna die or anything. But I liked the idea of a very long nap. I thought maybe if I woke up in about a year, everything would be okay.

The food is good here and I am eating now. To be honest it is better than my mother's cooking but I am not going to tell her that. She has been swell towards me since my "breakdown." That's what everyone calls it. They don't say it in front of me. I can hear them whisper it though in my room when they are off talking about me like I am not really present. The doctors say I have a case of depression. I have no idea what that means but my father once said it was when everyone was broke. I guess I am sort of broke. I feel okay but most days I don't feel like getting out of bed. My brother would say I am lazy but honestly I don't think it is that. I guess being "depressed" is like being sad all the time. If it was being without money I was sure not gonna last in Westport for too long.

I go to regular meetings here with other crack pots. They are not really crazy but most are really messed up. I mean I may be sad and took a bottle of aspirin and all but I am not loony. I am sort of surprised how many of them there are. There are even some my age. There is this one kid, I won't use his name because that is sort of against the rules, but he is in 5th grade here in Westport. He had a father who beat him. Beat him bad. Took a belt to his butt and I have seen the welts on his backside. It ain't pretty, trust me. So this kid got sick of trying to please his father all the time. He got the belt and tried to hang himself with it one morning. He wrapped the belt around the curtain rod and attempted to do himself in but the rod broke and he ended up smashing his head on the tub. He spent three days in the Norwalk Hospital and then came here.

There are a whole bunch of other sorts of weird people here too. Many just walk around talking to themselves but I ain't going to bore you with all the stories of all the loonies. You have mine and I guess that will have to be enough.

I am feeling better as each day goes by but I do miss being home and playing baseball. They have a 3 hole golf course out in front of this place and I have asked Mom to bring me my clubs. I doubt she will bring them as it would seem real loony for a young kid like me to be playing golf at the nut house. Someone might see me from Long Lots Road.

There is some talk about sending me to private school which would make me a rich Westport kid instead of a middle class goofball. I am not sure there are girls at such schools. Not that my experience is too great along those lines. Betsy taught me that. Girls are really creepier than boys. Or maybe it was just me. I may never know.

That finishes my summer and my assignment for the doctor. He isn't exactly normal himself but I won't bore you with that. So now I will just say I wrote this damn thing myself although I got help from my brother on some of the big words and all. He is being sort of nice for him. I guess a lot of people feel sorry for me but I don't really care. I am sort of looking forward to playing Babe Ruth baseball next summer. Even if I do go to private school I can always come back to Westport.

CPSIA information can be obtained at www.ICGtesting.com
Printed in the USA
BVOW081731110713

325683BV00001B/5/P

9 781478 704959